After you Returned

THE RAIDER BROTHERS

D.E. Haggerty

ISBN: 9789083677903

Also by D.E. Haggerty

Smuggler's Hideaway Series

Before It Was Love

After The Vows

While We Waited

All Along

Beyond The Hate

The Raider Brothers Series – a Smuggler's Hideaway Spin-off Series

Until It Was Real

For The Promise

From The Start

Only for the Season

Since You Arrived

After You Returned

The Cash & the Sinners Series

How to Date a Rockstar

How to Love a Rockstar

How to Fall For a Rockstar

How to Be a Rockstar's Boyfriend

How to Catch a Rockstar

The *Winter Falls* Series

My Forever Love

Forever For You

Just For Forever

Stay For Forever

Only Forever

The *Winter Falls ~ Dempsey Sisters* series

Meet Disaster

Meet Not

Meet Dare

Meet Hate

The *Winter Falls ~ Bragg Brothers* Series

Bragg's Truth

Bragg's Love

Perfect Bragg

Bragg's Match

Bragg's Christmas

The *Love will OUT* series

A Hero for Hailey

A Protector for Phoebe

A Soldier for Suzie

A Fox for Faith

A Christmas for Chrissie

A Valentine for Valerie

A Love for Lexi

The *Love in the Suburbs* series

About Face

At Arm's Length

Hands Off

Knee Deep

Other romantic comedies by D.E. Haggerty

Molly's Misadventures

Chapter 1

Miles – a surfer who still hasn't figured out how to rectify the biggest mistake he made in his life

Miles

I secure my surfboard under my arm before splashing through the waves onto the shore. I plant the board in the sand and lean over to shake out my hair. Water droplets fly everywhere.

"Hey! You're getting me all wet," Kai complains.

I smirk. "I know."

My brother shoves me. "You're such a child."

"Says the child who's shoving me."

My oldest brother, Eli, clears his throat. "Can you two behave for five minutes?"

"He started it," Kai and I respond simultaneously.

Rhett, another one of my brothers, groans. "Act your age."

I wrinkle my nose. "Sounds boring."

Zane sighs while Jaxon checks his watch. "Can I leave now?"

I roll my eyes at my brothers. Yes, more brothers. I have five of them – Eli, Rhett, Jaxon, Zane, and Kai. We used to be 'those

Raider brothers' as in the shit stirring, pranking, fun revelers. But not anymore.

All of my brothers have found love and they've become – gag – domesticated. Eli, Rhett, and Zane even have children. While Eli and Rhett's children were planned for, Zane's baby was a complete surprise. Some woman he doesn't remember dropped baby Adele on his doorstep and – boom! – instant dad.

Rhett throws an arm around Jaxon's shoulders. "No, you can't leave. It's the Smugglers' Blaze."

The Smugglers' Blaze isn't any old New Year's Eve bonfire. It's a glorified excuse for the entire island to gather on the sand, drink moonshine that should require a warning label, and pretend they're sending the year's mistakes up in smoke.

"I'm ready to say goodbye to this year," I mutter.

Watching all of my brothers fall in love while the woman I want won't give me the time of day has not been my idea of a fun year.

Rhett grins. "Let's do this."

He hands out shot glasses before pulling a bottle of moonshine out of his bag.

Jaxon fiddles with his glasses. "I thought we agreed to say goodbye to the year with my new Christmas whiskey."

Jaxon is the master distiller of *Buccaneer's Whiskey & Distillery,* the distillery Eli founded after becoming a billionaire. Eli insisted his brothers were the only people he wanted to manage the brewery with him, and now, we all work there.

Jaxon loves it. He couldn't wait to start developing whiskeys and moonshine. He's extremely anal about his work. The nerd. But he is freaking fabulous at his job.

Unlike me. I'm the sales manager and I don't suck at it but it's not the job I want to be doing. I should be traveling the world on the surfing pro tour. Instead, I'm stuck on this island working an office job.

Don't get me wrong. I surf as often as I can. I even give surfing lessons to tourists in the summer. But it's not the same as going pro – riding the biggest waves in the world while everyone watches.

My shoulder aches to remind me of why I'm trapped working an office job. I injured my rotator cuff at my first professional surfing event in Hawaii. I worked my ass off at rehab, but I never regained the strength needed to be a professional surfer.

"It's traditional to drink moonshine at the Smugglers' Blaze," Eli says before lifting his shot glass. "Here's to the ones who sank their ships, lost their hearts, and still showed up for last call.May next year bring smoother seas, stronger drinks, and fewer regrets — though not too few."

"Smugglers!" we shout before downing our shots.

Rhett quickly refills our glasses. "To bad ideas that turned into good stories, to moonshine that burned just right, and to the fools who keep coming back for more. May the new year find you not older, but wiser."

"To good stories!"

The moonshine burns as I drink the second shot but it doesn't stop me from holding out my glass for a refill.

"To another year of bad ideas, good liquor, and the kind of family you can't outrun — no matter how far you surf!" I shout before downing the third shot.

"I'm done," Kai announces. "I'm helping Harper at the *Rumrunner* booth."

I roll my eyes. Of course, he is. Harper is his girlfriend. She's also the owner of the speakeasy – *Rumrunner.* But the bar isn't open tonight since everyone on the island is on the beach. Instead, she set up a booth near the boardwalk to sell liquor until the crowd gets too rowdy and she shuts it down.

Eli rubs his hands together. "Time to light the bonfire."

I glance behind me at the fire structure. It's piled high with Christmas trees. It's tradition to take down your tree on the thirty-first of December and bring it to the beach. I didn't bring my tree. Mostly because I didn't have a Christmas tree. There's no sense decorating for the holiday when you're alone.

My stomach sours. Being alone is not my choice. Unfortunately, there's only one woman for me and she won't give me the time of day.

I really screwed up with Hazel. We were high school sweethearts, but when the chance arose to participate in a pro surfing event in Hawaii, I couldn't dump her fast enough. I didn't want to be tied down to this island.

Joke's on me. I ended up injured and returned to the island with my tail between my legs. I should have run to her and begged her for forgiveness. But I was a fool. Too ashamed of my behavior and upset about losing the career I'd always dreamed of to do the right thing.

The crowd begins to chant, and I force thoughts of the past away.

"Blaze it! Raise it! Rum can't faze it!" The crowd repeats as Eli makes his way to the pile of Christmas trees and driftwood.

"I'm getting my baby girl home before it gets dangerous," Zane announces before stomping toward the *Rumrunner* booth, where his girlfriend, Sloane, is helping Harper set up with his baby, Adele, strapped to her front.

At least, Eli, Rhett, and Jaxon aren't running away – yet. Someone hands Eli a wooden torch, and Rhett helps him light it.

"All right, you glorious bunch of rum-soaked misfits." Eli lifts the lit torch in the air. "It's time to torch the past and toast the future. Here's to bad ideas, good stories, and one hell of a hangover. Let's set this year on fire!"

"Set the year on fire! Set the year on fire!" the crowd chants as Eli throws the torch at the pile. It catches fire, and within seconds, Smugglers' Blaze is burning bright.

"Welp. I've done my duty. Time to get my family home." Eli searches the beach. He smiles when his gaze lands on Paisley and their baby daughter, Stephanie. He doesn't bother to say goodbye before making a beeline to them.

"If you get arrested, I'm not bailing you out until tomorrow morning," Rhett declares before making his way toward Dakota and their two children – Pearl and Mira.

"Yes, well." Jaxon clears his throat before backing away.

"I thought Blossom would enjoy the bonfire."

Unlike Jaxon, whose face can be found next to the entry for 'introvert' in the dictionary, his wife, Blossom, is an extrovert who loves fun. The two couldn't be more opposite.

"She didn't come. She isn't feeling well."

"She's not pregnant, is she?"

Jaxon fiddles with his glasses.

"Oh shit. I was joking." I hold out my hand. "Congrats, brother."

He shakes his head. "She's not pregnant. Yet."

I drop my hand. "I didn't know you were trying."

He shrugs. "We're not, not trying." He nods toward the boardwalk. "Anyway, I'm off. And you should get out of your wetsuit."

I glance down. I forgot I was wearing a wetsuit. I wear one so often, it's practically a second skin to me. But it's no fun having to pee while wearing one. And since I'm planning to do more drinking tonight, I should probably change.

I grab my board before making my way toward my surf shack. This is where I keep my surfboards and other equipment for giving surfing lessons. I also keep extra clothes in here.

I quickly change into warmer clothes. I grab a beer from the fridge before locking up and meandering toward the bonfire.

I scan the crowd. Almost every inhabitant from Smuggler's Hideaway is here. Except my brothers, who bailed early on me.

Last year, we closed this bonfire down. I also had the worst hangover on New Year's Day and nearly threw up in the ocean during the Salty Dip, but it was worth it.

Hands Off

Knee Deep

Other romantic comedies by D.E. Haggerty

Molly's Misadventures

Things are changing for the Raider brothers and I don't approve at all. With five brothers, I'm not used to being alone, but alone is exactly what I am.

My gaze catches on long, red hair. Hazel. Anticipation barrels through me as my fingers tingle with the desire to touch her.

I finish my beer and throw the bottle in the trash before strolling toward her.

Maybe I don't have to be alone this New Year's Eve after all.

Chapter 2

Hazel – a woman who should know better but is weak when it comes to Miles

Hazel

I groan as I try to roll over in bed, but I can't move. A heavy weight over my stomach anchors me in place. What the hell?

I pry my eyes open and the world immediately begins to spin while my stomach heaves. I slam my eyes shut before I throw up in bed.

Swimming mermaids in the sea. How much did I drink last night?

I flip through my memories. Yesterday was New Year's Eve. I went to the Smugglers' Blaze with my sisters, Scarlett and Sadie. Scarlett begged off early when her boyfriend, Weston, got off duty. And Sadie made herself scarce when Miles showed up.

Miles.

I didn't, did I? Please tell me I didn't drink too much and end up back in his bed. I'm not that big of an idiot. Or am I?

I pry my eyes open again and glance down at the weight on my stomach. Marauding pirates, I'd know this arm anywhere.

I am that big of an idiot.

There's obviously something wrong with me. What self-respecting woman lands in the bed of the man who dumped her years ago and is now only interested in her when he's been drinking and is horny?

Me. That's who.

Time to get the hell out of here before I'm forced to endure a morning after during which Miles does his best to get rid of me as fast as possible. It's bad enough I can't resist him but his embarrassment of me makes the situation even worse.

I grasp his arm and lift it. He fights me for a moment before rolling over to his other side. I use the opportunity to sneak out of bed. I gather my clothes from the floor before tiptoeing out of the room.

Once I'm in the hallway with the door shut behind me, I hurry to dress before rushing to the front door. I don't have any means of transportation, but Smuggler's Rest is a small town. It's a mere fifteen-minute walk to my apartment from here.

This isn't a walk of shame. Mostly because no one on the island is awake yet. It's nine a.m. on New Year's Day. Most of the town was at the Smugglers' Blaze last night until the wee hours of the morning.

My stomach dips and weaves as I walk. I place a hand over it, but it does nothing to combat the nausea. At least the Salty Dip – the annual New Year's Day swim in the ocean – doesn't start until noon. I can grab a few more hours of sleep and hopefully not be too hungover when I meet my family at the beach.

I feel twenty times better after another two hours of sleep in my own bed. And a shower doesn't hurt either. But when I try to drink some coffee, my stomach revolts. Guess I'm not completely out of the woods yet.

I dress in warm fleece clothing before grabbing a beach towel and exiting my apartment. I notice my neighbor, Melanie, waiting for the elevator and whirl around to make my way to the stairs. The last person in the world I want to question me about my activities last night is my prudish neighbor.

The beach is a mere five minutes away. I love living near the water. Of course, on an island the size of Smuggler's Hideaway, the water is never far away.

"Hazel!" Sadie shouts before rushing toward me. "You made it."

My brow wrinkles. "Of course, I made it. The Salty Dip is a Harris family tradition."

My sister throws her arm over my shoulders. "I thought you might be otherwise occupied." She wiggles her eyebrows.

I shove her away. "Knock it off or I'll tell everyone on the island about how you're falling in love with your pen pal."

She glares at me. "You're the one who tricked me into signing up for the military pen pal program."

"Do you want to go there? Because tricking you was seriously mild payback considering how much the goat you smuggled into my apartment shat. Do you know how long it takes to get rid of the smell of goat shit?"

"You shouldn't have called the police on me."

I roll my eyes. "I didn't call the police on you."

She fists her hands on her hips. "Why the hell did they show up at my door at 3 a.m. if you didn't call them?"

I shrug. "Scarlett's dating a cop. Ask her."

"Don't think—"

"Sadie! Hazel!" Our brother, Thomas, yells as he walks our way with our other brother, Ian.

"Baa!"

I stare down at the sheep walking behind them. "Did you bring a sheep to the Salty Dip?"

"Sheepwreck Sally loves to swim," Thomas insists.

I blow out a breath. "She's a sheep. Sheep don't swim."

Sadie giggles. "At least they didn't cause a traffic jam this time."

I groan. My brothers are sheep farmers. They're also shit stirrers who thought it'd be funny to 'test' Weston and his sheep herding skills by letting the sheep wander all over the island.

"What are you up to?"

My question is met with wide, innocent eyes. As if. Thomas and Ian haven't been innocent since they discovered moonshine in their teens and decided to race tractors through the fields. I have never seen Dad's face get that red. And I never want to again.

"Fine. Have your fun. But I am not bailing you out of jail again."

Ian rolls his eyes. "Are you ever going to let it go? You bailed us out of jail one time."

"I was in the middle of my final exam for physiology. I nearly failed."

Thomas grins. "But you didn't, Sis, because you're brilliant."

"Flatter me all you want. I am still not bailing you out of jail."

"Bailing him out of jail for what?" Weston asks as he and Scarlett join us.

"Our sister had to fall in love with a cop," Thomas mutters.

"We didn't do anything!" Ian shouts.

Weston groans. "And here I thought you two were done testing me when you didn't get up to any trouble last night."

Scarlett giggles. "Didn't get into trouble? Did you miss the gossip? These two yahoos raced sheep down Main Street."

Weston holds up his hands. "Don't tell me. I don't want to know. I wasn't on duty."

Thomas clears his throat. "When do you go back on duty?"

Weston squeezes Scarlett's hand. "You're lucky I love you, Precious."

She beams at him. "I am lucky."

"You're going to be even luckier later."

Ian gags. "Don't talk about having sex with our sister."

Thomas nods. "Gross."

Weston smirks. "You don't want to hear about the time—"

Scarlett slaps a hand over his mouth. "Don't you dare."

He pries her fingers away. "I would never, but you have to let me mess with your brothers."

"Or you could take the higher road and ignore them."

Weston barks out a laugh. "Not happening."

"What's going on?" Dad booms as he walks up to us with Mom. "Why are you standing around on the boardwalk? It's nearly time for the Salty Dip."

He herds us onto the beach where a crowd has already gathered.

"I'm going to win best costume this year," Thomas says as he removes his sweats and throws them on the ground.

I blink when his outfit is revealed. "Are you Little Bo Peep?"

"And I brought props." He whistles and Sheepwreck Sally meanders toward him.

Weston grunts. "If the sheep shits on the beach, you're picking it up."

"I thought you were off duty," Ian says.

Thomas bats his eyelashes at Weston. "Can't you use your 'sheep whispering energy' to ensure Sheepwreck Sally behaves?"

Weston growls. "I never said I have 'sheep whispering energy'."

"You didn't?" Sadie digs her phone out of her pocket. "Because I have a recording of someone who sounds suspiciously like you claiming he has 'sheep whispering energy' and can herd sheep with saltine crackers."

Weston wags his finger at her. "You can't use recordings made after a bottle of moonshine is drunk."

"You probably shouldn't have claimed you could drink my brothers under the table," Scarlett mutters.

"Lesson learned."

Dad claps his hands. "Are we going to stand around here gossiping like a bunch of women all day, or are we going to swim?"

I flip off my sweatshirt and push down my sweatpants.

Sadie scoffs. "How original. You're a mermaid on Smuggler's Hideaway."

"You can be sarcastic all you want, but I'm winning the fastest dip this year."

The person who swims to the buoy and back the fastest wins a prize. I've come close to winning several times but this year is my year.

"You want to win because this year's prize is a gift basket from *Buccaneer's Whiskey & Distillery*. The distillery where Miles works."

I glare at her. If she brings up how I spent the night with Miles, she'll wish the worst revenge I ever committed was signing her up for a pen pal.

"Miles?" Dad grumbles. To say my dad isn't a fan of my ex-boyfriend is putting it mildly.

"Now, now, dear." Mom pats his arm.

"Have you been hanging around that boy again?"

A whistle blows. "Swimmers, take your marks."

Saved by the whistle. "I'll see you after I win." I rush off to the starting line before Dad has a chance to stop me.

No way, no how, am I discussing Miles with my dad. My cheeks heat as embarrassment hits me. I am such a fool for that man.

Chapter 3

I probably shouldn't have smirked.

Two months later

Miles

I glare at my phone when it rings. *Eli calling.* I contemplate ignoring him, but there's no delaying the inevitable. My brothers won't let me ignore them. They'll drag me by my ear if they have to. I'm not exaggerating. It wouldn't be the first time.

"Hey, Eli."

"Where are you?"

At home. Where I want to be.

When I don't answer, he sighs. "Shall I pick you up?"

"If I have to go, you do, too," Jaxon shouts.

Jaxon hates family occasions. He doesn't hate the Raider family. But he finds group outings stressful. He's a nerd who's proud to be an introvert. Being married to Blossom has made him more open to social occasions, but he's still an introvert. All of which to say, if he's with Eli, he's going to *Rumrunner* and there's no way I can bow out gracefully.

"Fine. Pick me up."

My house is in Smuggler's Rest. I can easily walk to *Rumrunner.* Hell, I can – and have – crawled back home from there on occasion.

But I'm happy to hitch a ride since I don't want to go out tonight. Not when I know Hazel will be at the bar.

If you look up mistake in the dictionary, you'll find a picture of me. I never should have let Hazel sneak out of my house on New Year's Day. I wasn't sleeping. I heard her crawl out of bed and tiptoe out of the room.

Why didn't I say anything? Why did I lay there and pretend I was sleeping?

And now Hazel scurries the other way every time she sees me. I'm practically banned from the *Smuggler's Cove Restaurant,* where she works part-time as the hostess. Whenever I enter, she says 'nope' and walks away.

The owner is beyond pissed with me. She asked me not to come around until my 'issues' with Hazel are solved. It's kind of hard to solve an issue when the other person won't stay in the same room as you.

I hear a honk and drag myself outside. Eli's SUV is already full but I squeeze in between Blossom and Jaxon.

"Why can't you sit on the other side of me?" Jaxon asks.

"And miss you complaining?"

"I want to sit next to my wife."

"It's okay, nerd boy," Blossom says. "We'll get there faster if we don't have to all change seats."

Blossom isn't a nerd or an introvert the way Jaxon is, but she is obsessed with time management. She's allergic to being late. Seriously, she breaks out in a rash when there's even a possibility of her not arriving on time.

I throw my arm around her. "And this way, we can become better acquainted."

Jaxon growls. "Keep your hands off my wife."

Blossom giggles. "He's riling you up to get his mind off how Hazel will be at the bar."

I glare at her. "You're my least favorite sister-in-law."

"Technically, I'm your only sister-in-law since none of the other Raider brothers have gotten married yet. Engaged doesn't count."

I scowl at the reminder of how we are no longer those shit-stirring Raider brothers having fun, attending Mermaid karaoke, playing pranks on each other, and drinking way too much moonshine. I miss those days. It's no fun drinking by yourself, and the amount of pranks has slowed to a crawl.

We arrive at the bar and everyone piles out. Zane is waiting for us at the end of the alleyway with his baby, Adele. Rhett and Dakota are standing next to him.

"Good," Zane says. "You're here."

"I don't know why we're here," I whine.

He scowls at me. "I need your moral support."

"Whatever," I mutter and motion him forward.

We arrive at the entrance to the bar. *Rumrunner* is a speakeasy. You can't just walk in. Even if you are a native of Smuggler's Hideaway.

Zane knocks on the door and the bouncer, Trent, opens the sliding peephole in the middle of the door.

"Uh oh. The Raider brothers have arrived," he mutters before opening the door for us to enter.

Landlubbers have to solve a riddle to enter the speakeasy, but as locals, we can enter without solving the riddle. Although the riddles aren't difficult. The answer is usually a mermaid, or a smuggler, or Prohibition. All the things Smuggler's Hideaway is famous for.

We enter the bar and Zane makes a beeline for the bartender to ask for Sloane, who works here. He totally fucked up with her and she left his ass. I would have left him, too. But he realized he messed up and now he's here to beg her forgiveness.

Which is why all of us brothers are at the bar with him. Whenever a Raider needs support, we come running. No matter how much we may want to avoid a certain red-headed mistake.

We gather in a corner of the bar to watch the reunion. And to heckle if the chance arises. I help my brothers shove tables together until there's enough room for all of the Raider family.

"I need a drink." I take everyone's orders before making my way to the bar.

On the way there, my gaze snags on red hair. Hazel must be a siren because my feet automatically change directions until I'm standing in front of her.

"What do you want?"

Her anger does nothing to detract from her beauty. On the contrary, her green eyes are entrancing as they blaze with fury. And wrinkling her nose only makes it more adorable. I love the freckles that spread across her nose and cheeks. I've kissed every one of them as well as those not visible when she's dressed.

And then there are those pouty, pink lips. Her frown can't diminish how sexy her mouth is. I love tracing those lips with my tongue before melding my mouth to hers.

"Hello?" She snaps her fingers in my face before I have the chance to drop my gaze to her body, which is curvy in all my favorite places. "I asked you a question. What do you want?"

What do I want? I want to throw her over my shoulder and drag her out of this speakeasy. But based on how she's fisting her hands at her hips, she'd probably punch me in the face if I tried.

"Can we talk?" I ask instead.

"Talk?" She snorts. "You don't want to talk. You never want to talk. You want to get into my pants and then forget all about it the next day."

"Not true." I can never forget about Hazel. I've spent the past weeks laying in bed imagining how it felt to have her in my arms again on New Year's Eve. How good she smelled. How crazy she goes for me when I kiss her lips.

My cock twitches. It remembers how it feels to be buried inside her.

"Not true? You're a liar. You're only interested in me when you're drunk. The rest of the time, you ignore me."

Wrong. When I'm drunk is the only time I dare to approach her. When I'm sober, I know better than to court her wrath. Usually.

"I'm not drunk now."

She scans the room until her gaze falls on the Raider table, which is empty of drinks since I was supposed to order them. They can get their own drinks. I'm busy here.

"Fine." She crosses her arms over her chest and I can't avoid dropping my gaze to her cleavage. It's magnificent. She's magnificent.

I reach for her and she scoots backwards. "I didn't give you permission to touch me."

I smirk. "You always do in the end."

Her green eyes flare with ire before she shouts, "Get away from me, Miles Raider!"

She doesn't wait for me to move. She runs away. And I give chase.

She plows through the crowd to the back hallway. She hurries past the ladies' room to the storage room. Shit. She's going for the secret exit.

"Wait!"

She glances over her shoulder. Her hair flies behind her and her cheeks are flushed from the effort. Damn. She's beautiful. She steals my breath away.

She enters the storage room and I nearly crash into the door when she slams it shut. I try to push it open, but it doesn't move more than an inch. She must have blocked it with crates of beer.

I pound my fist on the door. "Hazel! Let me in!"

She doesn't answer. I hear the telltale whirling sound of the secret exit opening up. She's getting away. I press my shoulder against the door and shove until the opening is big enough for me to slip through.

But I'm too late. The secret exit is wide open but there's no sign of Hazel.

That went well.

Chapter 4

For the last time. It's a wall rack, not a torture device.

Hazel

I smile as I switch on the lights for my physical therapy practice. It isn't much. A slightly wide entrance I use as a reception area, a small room with a treatment table, and a larger room propped full with all of the rehabilitation equipment I could afford.

I would love to work as a therapist full-time, but there are simply not enough clients on this small island. We get a ton of tourists in the summer but most tourists don't need physical therapy while they're on vacation.

I get by because I have a second job at a restaurant. But I don't know how long I can continue to work at *Smuggler's Cove Restaurant.* Every year, the waitresses get younger and more flirty with the customers. While I want to shove a fork into the eye of every man who thinks it's okay to leer at my ass.

Stupid men. Stupid Miles. He's the king of stupid men.

I am done with him. He doesn't want to talk. He wants to have sex and then forget all about me the next morning. Well, no more. I am not a booty call. I deserve more. Way more than Miles Raider can ever give.

The bell over the door rings. "Hello," a woman shouts.

I frown. My appointment isn't with a woman.

I peek into the hallway. "What are you doing here, Maya?"

Caleb – who is a patient of mine – walks inside behind her and sighs. "Sorry, Hazel. She insisted on joining me today."

I raise my eyebrows. "Insisted? Are you injured, Maya?"

"She's fine unless dying of curiosity is a real thing," he mutters.

Curiosity? Uh oh.

I love Smuggler's Hideaway. I love being close to the beach. I love knowing most of the inhabitants. I love how safe it is. I love how quirky it is. I love the mermaid lore. I love the Prohibition stories about moonshine.

What I don't love is how everyone gossips as if it's a national sport. An incredibly competitive national sport. And it's even worse. The gossipers appear to have their sights set on me.

"Curiosity? Are you interested in becoming a physical therapist?" I ask because I am not feeding the gossipers. They'd have better luck speaking to a mermaid.

Her nose wrinkles. "Would I have to interact with other people?"

Maya is shy. As the financial manager for the local brewery, *Five Fathoms Brewing*, she doesn't have to deal with strangers much. Which is exactly how she prefers it. How she ever convinced Caleb – who was determined to keep her in the friendzone – to give her a chance is beyond me.

I giggle. "The whole point of therapy is to help other people, so interacting with people is kind of necessary. You'd have to touch them, too."

Caleb growls. "Maya is not touching strange men."

Holy smugglers caught in a storm. Caleb is one sexy dude but when he gets all protective over his woman? Wowzer.

I wouldn't mind a man over six feet tall with bulging muscles, blond hair, and blue eyes wanting to protect me from the world. Miles certainly doesn't protect me from anyone or anything.

He's also not my man. Good reminder.

"If you're not here to check out a day in the life of a physical therapist, why are you here?" I ask Maya.

She clears her throat. "Rumor has it—"

I hold up my hand to stop her. "Nope. No way. Not happening."

She widens her eyes as if she's all innocent. As if. Maya and her girlfriends, who own the brewery together, are the least innocent women on the island. Their troublemaking rivals the Raider brothers.

And now I'm thinking about Miles again. He's not Rome. Not all roads should lead to him. But here I am. Steering my mind toward him every chance I get.

"I told you to let it go," Caleb grumbles. "You just had a baby. Lucy should be keeping you busy enough."

Maya sighs. "I love Lucy. She's the best baby in the world."

"Congratulations!"

She smiles and all the love she has for her baby and her husband shines through. A ball tightens in my stomach. I ignore it. I refuse to be jealous. Maya and Caleb deserve to be happy. Especially after Caleb came home injured from a deployment to some faraway, unknown country.

"Thanks. I'm a lucky girl."

"Where's Lucy now?"

"With Caleb's mom. I'll probably have to fight her to get her back."

Caleb frowns. "The last time my parents babysat, they weren't home when we arrived to pick up Lucy. They weren't ready to say goodbye, so they took her on a road trip."

Maya slaps his chest. "It wasn't a road trip. They were home before it got dark."

"Still. Mom would kidnap Lucy if she didn't know I'd track her down."

Maya rolls her eyes. "Yes, we all know how Mr. Former Army can track anyone down."

"Speaking of Mr. Former Army." I motion toward my rehab room. "We should get started."

"Where do you want me?"

Caleb is the ideal patient. He never whines or complains. He does the exercises I assign him to do at home. He doesn't really need to come to therapy anymore as he can continue to rehab on his own, but I'm thankful for his weekly visits.

I point to the wall bar. "Let's start with some stretches."

"Awesome. We haven't used the torture machine for some time."

I giggle. "You refer to all of my equipment as torture machines."

He shrugs. "If the peg leg fits…"

Maya scowls. "You do not have a peg leg."

"It's just a saying, bunny."

"I don't want you making fun of your injury."

"It's hardly an injury anymore," I say. "Caleb's leg is stronger than the legs of most of the smugglers on this island."

"Because most of the smugglers drink too much moonshine and beer," Caleb says.

"How about Miles?" Maya asks. "Does he have strong legs? Do surfers have strong legs?"

I am not answering any questions about Miles's physique. My body is also not getting warm and tingly, remembering how strong Miles's legs are. How he can easily balance me against a wall with his legs without breaking into a sweat. Nope. Not thinking those thoughts at all.

"Surfers in general have strong legs. It's necessary for balance and performing maneuvers. The upper body is also worked hard through paddling."

She rubs her hands together. "In other words, Miles has great legs and a strong upper body."

"Tell you what. I'll answer your question…"

She grins but I haven't finished yet.

"If you can do a pull-up on the wall bar."

"A pull-up?"

"Do you need me to demonstrate?"

I start walking to the wall bar but Caleb shoos me away. "I'll demonstrate."

I cross my arms over my chest. "By all means. Proceed."

He jumps to the highest rung of the bar and I nod in satisfaction. He used both legs evenly. He didn't favor his uninjured right leg. He folds his legs behind him and I evaluate the bending motion of his left leg. Looking good.

"One." Caleb executes a perfect pull-up. "Two. Three."

Maya leans close to whisper in my ear. "Should I tell him I know what a pull-up is? Or stand here and watch how sexy his biceps are?"

I point to the corner of my mouth. "You're drooling."

She motions to Caleb. "Have you seen him? Of course, I'm drooling."

"Ten!" He announces before jumping off the wall bar. He bends his knees evenly as he lands. He doesn't wobble in the least.

"Looking good, Caleb. I hate to say it, but I don't think you need therapy anymore."

"But you have the best equipment."

I roll my eyes. "You work at *Hideaway Haven Resort.* I happen to know Hudson equipped the gym with every piece of equipment a professional sports person could possibly need."

"Hudson's a former NFL player. He wants to keep in shape," Caleb says.

"Wants to keep in shape or wants his former team to come and visit him?" Maya asks.

Caleb scowls at her. "You promised you could keep a secret."

Secret? My curiosity is piqued. "What secret?"

Maya mimes zipping her lips.

Caleb sighs. "You might as well tell her before you burst. Hazel can keep a secret."

I form the Girl Scout salute. "I promise not to tell."

Maya unzips her lips. "It's not official yet. But there might be a team of football players staying at the resort this summer during training camp."

"Cool."

Smuggler's Hideaway is always full of tourists in the summer. And the *Hideaway Haven Resort* often hosts famous people. Movie stars, sports heroes, and rock stars have all been guests at the resort.

Maya's phone rings. She frowns before digging it out of her pocket. "Shoot. It's Sophia. I better get back to the office."

She rushes toward the door but Caleb captures her wrist and drags her back. He plants a kiss on her lips. "Love you, Bunny."

She smiles up at him with stars in her eyes. "Love you, too, soldier."

When she doesn't move, Caleb smiles at her. "Don't you need to get to work?"

"Oh, right. Yes. See you at home."

They're more adorable than a pod of mermaids frolicking in the sea. The ball in my stomach tightens until it's a knot. An uncomfortable, painful knot I can't ignore.

I want what they have. I thought I found it in high school when I gave my heart to Miles.

I was wrong. Miles didn't hesitate to throw me away the second he thought he was going to be a famous pro surfer. Asshole.

Chapter 5

If this is what I get for being a hero, I'm done with heroics.

Miles

I whistle as I open my surf shack. Early morning is my favorite time to surf. The water is glassy, creating clean peaks. And there aren't many tourists around yet.

This morning is an exceptional morning to surf. The swells are at least ten seconds, creating powerful, less choppy waves. And the offshore wind is blowing from the beach toward the ocean, creating cleaner, more organized waves.

My body hums with excitement as I grasp a few surfboards. I have a group of five students this morning. It's their fifth lesson. We've been out on the water before but only to ride small foam waves. I'm hoping today is the day they learn how to stand up on their own and catch some real waves.

There's nothing more satisfying than watching a person who didn't know how to paddle a few days ago pop up on their board and ride a wave. I scowl. Nothing more satisfying? I can think of a few hundred more satisfying things. They all begin and end with Hazel.

"Hey!" Natalie greets.

"Good morning." I smile at her and her friends. "Are you ready to ride some waves?"

Barbara bites her bottom lip. "I don't know. I'm struggling with popping up."

"We can practice on the beach."

Carly elbows her. "I'm done practicing on the beach. I'm ready to ride those waves."

Jolie and Etta nod in agreement.

I rub my hands together. "Let's review ocean safety and wave selection before we get into the water."

Jolie groans. "We've heard you lecture about ocean safety and wave selection every morning. I think we get it."

I rest my hands on my hips. "I guess you already checked the weather this morning, then."

Her nose wrinkles. "Checked the weather? You check the weather for us."

"I won't always be here. Today is your fifth and last lesson."

Etta bats her eyelashes at me. "But you'll be around here to help us if we need it."

I bite back a groan. These ladies have been flirting with me since the first minute of the first lesson. My refusal to engage hasn't deterred them one bit.

"I'm not always here," I lie. I try to surf every morning before going to work. "And when you return home, you'll need to check the weather on your own."

Jolie giggles. "We live in Omaha. There's not a whole lot of surfing in Nebraska."

"We're going home in two days," Natalie adds. "You should join us for drinks at the *Bootlegger* bar tonight."

"I'll think about it."

I have no interest in having drinks with these women. Especially not at *Bootlegger,* which is full of tourists – mostly college students celebrating Spring Break – this time of year. But I know better than to say no. They'll badger me until I change my mind. I've danced this dance before.

"In the meantime, it's time to surf."

I summarize our last lessons about reading the waves and maintaining balance, and how to pop up on the board before I hand out the surfboards before we make our way into the ocean.

"We want to paddle past the impact zone. Who remembers what the impact zone is?" I ask as we begin to paddle.

"The breaking waves," Natalie answers.

"Correct." I nod in her direction as I continue to paddle. "We want to reach the line-up where we'll wait for the unbroken waves."

"I don't know why we had to take surfing lessons during Spring Break," Barbara mutters. "Everyone else is still sleeping off their hangovers, and we're out here working hard."

"You need to work on your upper body strength," Carly says. "You barely made it through two strength training classes before you quit."

"The class was at six in the morning. I'm surprised I lasted two classes."

Carly rolls her eyes. "You act as if six is the middle of the night."

She paddles through the waves with ease. Her upper body is well-developed. She obviously didn't skip any of those strength training classes.

My body has no interest in Carly and her muscular physique. It's far more interested in curvy bodies. One curvy body in particular – Hazel's.

I need to stop obsessing over a woman who has no interest in me. Who runs away from every encounter with me. Who hates me.

The smuggler knows I've tried. I went to *Bootlegger* twice this week but I couldn't manage to drum up interest in any of the women who flirted with me. My cock has gone into hibernation and I have no idea when it's going to wake up again.

I reach the line-up and wait for the five women to join me. Carly is first, while Barbara is last.

"All right, ladies. It's time to show me what you've learned this week. I want you to choose a wave and try to ride it. Don't be discouraged if you need a few tries before you manage it. Surfing is a brand-new skill, and like all skills, practice makes perfect."

"I'm going first!" Carly shouts before paddling toward a wave. I watch as she pops up without any difficulties and rides the wave for a few seconds before crashing.

"One guess whose idea it was to do surfing lessons," Barbara mutters. "I wanted to learn how to mix margaritas, but no, we're in the ocean at the crack of dawn instead."

"Stop complaining. I saw the teacher of the margarita class. He can't hold a candle to Miles." Natalie winks at me.

I motion toward the approaching wave. "Your turn."

"I got this."

Unfortunately, her confidence is stronger than her ability to pop up on the board. She falls to the side before diving into the water.

"Phew," Jolie says. "I won't look bad if I crash and burn."

"This isn't a test," I tell her. "No one's grading you today."

"Good thing," she mutters. "I don't want to ruin my perfect grade point average."

Off she goes. She manages to pop up but wobbles once she's standing and barely manages a few feet before falling into the water.

"I'm next," Etta declares before smoothly paddling toward the upcoming wave. She appears confident. Rightfully so. She pops up without any issues and rides the wave while shouting for joy.

"Etta has had surfing lessons before," Barbara says. "But she doesn't want Carly to know. No one beats Carly when it comes to sports."

"You ready?" I motion to where a wave is forming.

"I guess so."

I frown at her lack of confidence. Confidence is important when performing any sport but especially a sport that could literally drown you.

I keep a careful watch on Barbara as she tries to pop up. Even from this distance, I notice how her arms and legs shake. This is not a good sign.

I don't have a good feeling about this. I begin to paddle in her direction.

She wobbles and starts to fall, but instead of diving into the water, she slips and her head slams into the board before she goes under.

Shit. Shit. Shit.

I paddle as hard as I can. The waves crash over me, but I ignore them as I continue to push myself.

"Barbara!" I shout when I reach the board. She still hasn't emerged from the water. Crap. Was she knocked unconscious?

"Barbara!" I shout again while untangling my surfboard leash from my leg and ankle. I find the Velcro strap on the leash cuff and loosen it before pulling it open and sliding the cuff off my ankle.

I grasp Barbara's surfboard leash with my left hand and dive into the water. I follow the leash until I reach her body.

Crap. She's unconscious, and her leash is tangled in seaweed. I yank on the cord but it's good and stuck.

My lungs burn, but I don't have time to surface for oxygen. Barbara's been underwater too long.

I grasp the cord with both hands. This is going to hurt. The rotator cuff of my right shoulder still aches six years after the injury. I grit my teeth and pull with all of my might.

The cord gives way and Barbara's body floats to the surface. I roll her onto her stomach, wrap an arm around her, and begin swimming to shore.

When I reach the shallow water, a lifeguard rushes toward me. "I've got her from here."

I release Barbara and crawl to the beach, where I collapse on my back. My shoulder burns from the pain. I push it down.

Once I've caught my breath, I stand and stumble toward the lifeguard. He has Barbara on her side and she's throwing up ocean water. Relief at her being alive nearly has me tumbling to my knees. I lock my legs to keep steady.

I hear sirens and turn to watch an ambulance stop at the edge of the beach. The paramedics jump out and rush toward us. A police car arrives seconds later.

Weston, Hazel's brother-in-law, steps out of the vehicle before sauntering my way.

"What happened?"

"He saved her life!" Natalie shouts.

"Good job." Weston slaps me on the shoulder and pain explodes. "You okay, Miles?"

"My rotator cuff," I say through gritted teeth.

I don't need to say more. Everyone on the island knows what happened to me in Hawaii at the pro surfing competition.

"Come on. I'll drive you to the hospital."

I want to argue. To tell him I'll be okay. But I'd be lying.

So much for a beautiful morning.

Chapter 6

I never should have left home today.

Hazel

I hum as I arrange a fresh sheet on my treatment table. I have a new client coming in today. I don't know who it is or what injury they have but I don't care. I'm just thankful for another client.

The bell above the door rings. I check my outfit. No stains. My hair is braided to avoid any entanglements. I'm ready.

I enter the reception area and frown. "What are you doing here?"

"I thought you were expecting me." Miles grins.

With his tanned skin and blond hair with matching beard, he could be the poster boy for a surfer. Appropriate since the one thing he finds important in life is surfing.

"I'm expecting a new patient. Not an asshole."

"I am the new patient." He taps his chest and winces.

"What happened?" He opens his mouth to respond, but I hold up my hand to stop him. "Never mind. I don't need to know since I won't be treating you."

He sighs. "I know you hate me."

Ugh. I wish his words were true. If I could hate Miles, my life would be much, much easier.

"But I need help."

"I don't think me helping you is a good idea."

I'll get my hands on him and forget all about what an asshole he is. How the man doesn't know how to stick. I'll feel his smooth skin and those strong muscles and lose my mind. It's happened too many times already. I'm determined it won't happen again.

"But where else can I go? There aren't any other physical therapists on the island."

I cross my arms over my chest. "Not true. Hudson has a therapist at the resort."

The *Hideaway Haven Resort* is the epitome of luxury. The location is prime – on a pristine beach in an otherwise empty area of the island. The spacious cabin accommodations are high-end with fancy linens, premium entertainment systems, and private hot tubs on the patios.

There's also an on-site spa and fitness center, as well as indoor and outdoor pools, gourmet dining at the restaurant, and every activity you can imagine, from surfing lessons to parasailing to private beach dinners.

Miles shakes his head. "Hudson couldn't fill the therapist position."

My brow wrinkles. "He couldn't?"

I didn't bother applying for the position since I assumed Hudson would hire some fancy therapist with experience with sports teams. Hudson is a former NFL player and the whole reason for the therapist is to help any sports professionals vacationing at the resort.

"Not a whole lot of people want to move to Smuggler's Hideaway."

I scowl. "Idiots. Smuggler's Hideaway is the best place to live in the world."

I haven't actually seen much of the world, but my statement stands.

He smiles. "The island is pretty awesome."

I roll my eyes. "Which is why you couldn't wait to escape when you were twenty."

He sighs. "How long are you going to punish me for what I did?"

I clench my jaw. He still doesn't get it. It's been six years, and he is none the wiser. I'm not mad at him for dumping me before he left. Correction. I was mad about him dumping me. But I got over it.

What I'm mad about is how he returned to the island a month later and pretended I didn't exist. Until he drinks too much moonshine and drunk dials me. And I'm the fool who answers the phone. No, I'm the fool who used to answer the phone.

"I don't think I should be your therapist," I say instead of explaining myself to him. If he doesn't get what's wrong by now, he never will. Besides, what good will rehashing the past do? It's not as if Miles wants a second chance with me.

"Come on, Blaze."

Blaze? How dare he call me Blaze? Blaze is the nickname Miles gave me when we were in high school. When I loved him and thought he would love me forever. I was a naïve fool.

I growl. "My name isn't Blaze."

He clears his throat. "Hazel, I need you."

How I've longed for him to say those words. For him to need me the way I need him. No, not the way I need him. The way I needed him. Past tense. I'm over him. He's nothing to me now.

"You don't need me. You need a therapist. I can recommend someone on the mainland."

"Don't make me go to the mainland. I don't have an extra hour every time I need therapy to waste on driving."

I lift an eyebrow. "You don't? As far as I know, you don't exactly spend much time at your job at *Buccaneer's Distillery*."

"Low blow, Hazel. Low blow."

Crap on a seafood cracker. He's right. I shouldn't tease him about not enjoying a job he never wanted in the first place. It couldn't have been easy going from future surfing professional to sales manager at a distillery owned by your older brother.

He could have leaned on me. I would have been there for him. But he pretended I didn't exist instead.

I nearly slap my forehead. Why can't I stop thinking about the past?

"Sorry."

"It's fine. But I really do need your help. I injured my rotator cuff yesterday."

"What? The rotator cuff on your right shoulder?"

Flying mermaids caught in a fisher's net. His right rotator cuff is the entire reason his pro surfing career came to an abrupt halt.

He nods. "The very one."

"What happened?"

"One of my surfing students got knocked out and was tangled in seaweed. I needed all my strength to pull her out before she drowned."

I grasp my chest. "Oh my smuggler. Is she okay?"

"She's fine. She has a nasty cut on her forehead, but otherwise she's perfectly fine."

"Thanks to you."

He shrugs and his cheeks darken slightly. Dang it. He's adorable when he's embarrassed. How can I refuse to help him when he injured himself saving a woman's life? I can't punish him for being a hero.

I pat the treatment table. "Hop on, remove your shirt, and lay down."

His blue eyes sparkle. "You're going to help me?"

"Unless you make some stupid comment about me asking you to remove your shirt. In which case, you're going to wish your rotator cuff was the worst pain you have."

He grins. "I love it when you're salty."

I roll my eyes. "But you hate it when I add salt to your coffee."

"You added salt to Zane's coffee. I got caught in the crossfire."

"He's your younger brother and therefore your responsibility."

"The same way you're responsible for Thomas and Ian."

I snort. "No one can accept responsibility for those two yahoos. They actually brought a sheep to the Salty Dip and then got annoyed when Sheepwreck Sally wasn't allowed to enter the competition for best costume."

He chuckles. "Ian and Thomas haven't changed one bit."

At the reminder of how well he knows my brothers – they were the best of friends back when Miles and I were dating – my good humor vanishes.

I check the clock. "Come on. Your thirty-minute session will be over before we can begin at this rate."

Miles whips off his t-shirt and my gaze snags on his six-pack abs. My fingers tingle with the need to reach out and touch him. To trail my fingertips along the ridges of his muscles before my tongue tastes every inch of his chest. To scrape my nails through the smattering of hair on his lower chest.

He clears his throat and I force my gaze to his face. His blue eyes have darkened to nearly violet with passion, but to his credit, he doesn't smirk or make some juvenile comment.

"Hop up on the table and lie down."

I wait until he's settled before asking, "What did the doctor say?"

"The tear isn't bad enough for surgery, but I need therapy and to modify my activity."

"No surfing."

He sighs. "No surfing."

I reach for him but stop. "Is it okay if I touch you?"

"Do your worst."

The second my hands touch him, I receive a jolt. I don't jump. I'm used to how electric it feels whenever we touch. Even after all these years, a single touch has my nervous system on high alert and my nipples tingling with anticipation.

Calm down, nipples. Nothing will be happening here.

I prod his shoulder and Miles sucks in a breath. I stop. "Did I hurt you?"

"No," he grits out.

"Your muscles are tight. I'm going to give you a soft tissue massage to loosen you up. You should be applying ice therapy, and I'll make a list of stretches for you to perform to prevent stiffness."

He groans. "I know the deal."

"I'm sorry, Miles."

"Not your fault." He squeezes my hip quickly. The second he releases me, I miss his heat. I want his hands on me. I want his heat enveloping me. This is why I didn't want to be his therapist.

Miles is catnip to me and I'm the horny cat who keeps coming back for more, no matter how much she gets hurt after every encounter.

I lather my hands with lotion before beginning the soft tissue massage. "How are your brothers doing? Is it true they all found love?"

I know it's true. You can't keep anything a secret on Smuggler's Hideaway. But I need to keep my mind on anything else but how I'm touching Miles's skin. How his abs are contracting with every move I make.

"I blame Eli. He started everything."

Relief fills me as Miles regales me with the stories of how his brothers fell in love. He isn't pushing me the way he usually does. He's letting me retreat.

Maybe I can be his therapist after all.

I glance down his body and notice the hard bulge tenting his pants.

Or maybe not.

Chapter 7

I really should have read that email.

Miles

I groan as I sit in my chair in my office at the distillery. My shoulder is fucking killing me. As much as I loved feeling Hazel's hands on me yesterday – my cock was especially appreciative – her massage didn't relieve the pain.

I hate this. Even after surgery and extensive therapy, my shoulder remains weak.

I glance around my office. If it weren't weak, I wouldn't be here.

I force those depressing thoughts away and switch on my computer. I type in my password but it's incorrect. This time, I slow down and make sure I don't make a mistake as I type in the password. Still incorrect.

What in the name of smuggling Prohibitionists is going on?

I've had the same password since I was a teenager. I know I typed it correctly.

"Zane!" I shout my brother's name.

"You rang." He grins as he saunters into my office, confirming he's the one who messed with my computer. He never would have rushed over here otherwise.

"What did you do?"

He bats his eyelashes. "Whatever do you mean?"

"Are we having a meeting?" Kai asks as he joins us.

I guess it's 'prank Miles time' since Kai shouldn't be anywhere near our offices. His office is on the other side of the building, where the distilling happens since he's the operations manager for *Buccaneer's Whiskey & Distillery.*

I rub a hand over my forehead where I can feel a headache forming. "No, we're not having a meeting. What did you do to my computer?"

Kai grasps his chest. "Your computer? Why would I mess with your computer?"

"Because you think you can win the prank war despite neglecting pranks for months while you were wooing Harper."

The Raider Brothers hold a prank war every year. Except last year, when my brothers were too busy falling in love to pull any pranks. I should have been a shoo-in to win, but Eli declared the prank war would last two years instead of one. Fine by me. I'll win this prank war either way.

Kai gasps. "I have never neglected pranks. How dare you!"

I motion to my computer. "Can you fix it? I don't have time for this shit today."

"You don't have time for this shit?" Zane asks. "What else are you going to do? It's not as if you can surf anytime soon."

"Thanks for the reminder, asshole," I mutter.

"I'm not the one who decided to play hero."

"I like Miles the hero," Kai says. "If you can't surf, you'll be around more often."

I roll my eyes. "I'm around all the time as it is. We see each other every day at work and most weekends at Mom's house or some related Raider brothers event."

Zane raises his eyebrow. "Every day at work?"

I glare at him. "Don't you start with me, Mr. Marketing Manager. Until Adele came into your life, you were gone even more than me. And when you were gone, you were gone to some far-flung place where no one could reach you."

"But now I'm a family man."

Rub it in, why don't you? He has the woman he's been drooling over for years, whereas I had the woman I want and lost her.

Jaxon peeks into my office. "You ready?"

My brow wrinkles. "Ready for what?"

"Dude." Zane shakes his head. "You really have been gone from the office too much if you don't know what's happening today."

"What's happening today?"

"I am not using a wheelchair!" Henry shouts from the reception area.

Kai chuckles. "I don't know why Harper bothers to push her father to use a wheelchair. He hates it. I better go check on father and daughter before they kill each other."

Jaxon glances at his watch. "We should all go. The ceremony should begin in one minute."

"What ceremony?"

He leaves my office without answering. Kai and Zane follow him. I can't exactly get any work done without the use of my computer and trail after them.

Instead of going in the direction of the reception area, we turn left toward the distillery. But before we enter the distillery, Jaxon stops at a door to the storage area. The door is open. Weird. The door is never open. Eli loses his mind if one of us forgets to lock up the storage.

I have no idea what he thinks is going to happen to the supplies in a locked distillery on an island where the crime rate is nearly non-existent. Assuming you don't include streaking or accidentally causing fires as crimes.

"Uncle Kai!" Pearl – Rhett and Dakota's oldest child – yells before barreling into my baby brother. He picks her up and whirls her around.

I peek inside the room and notice it's now decorated as a nursery and all of my nieces – apparently the Raider brothers are incapable of creating boys – are here.

"What the hell is going on?"

"Uncle Miles said a bad word." Pearl holds her hand out. "Dollar for the swear jar."

I pretend to slap a dollar in her hand.

"No faking. You owe me!"

"Send me an invoice," I say before asking Kai, "Why is the distillery suddenly full of Raider children?"

"This is the nursery."

"The nursery? Since when do we have a nursery at the distillery?"

Rhett stands next to me with baby Mira in his arms. "You were at the meeting when we agreed to review the issue."

I vaguely remember some talk of a nursery. "Review the issue is one thing." I motion to the room. "This is not a review."

"I sent a proposal to everyone. You had the chance to comment on the idea."

I rub my forehead. I don't remember receiving a proposal.

"This is what happens when you don't read your emails," Dakota sings as she steals Mira from Rhett's arms. Dakota is Eli's assistant and knows everything happening in the office – including my refusal to read emails.

"Hey!" Rhett chases after her. "I hardly held her for a second."

Kai sets Pearl on the ground before coming to stand next to me. "You have to admit. It's a good idea."

"I do? I don't have children. This is a huge cost with no benefit for me."

He shrugs. "You should have complained when you had the chance."

In other words, I should have read the email. In my defense, I do read most of my emails. The ones from the bars, restaurants, and resorts that we sell our whiskeys and moonshine to. And our distributors to coordinate shipping.

I've never lost a shipment or had one be delayed. And I always make sure contracts are in place before any Buccaneer's products arrive at a sales point.

But I missed the email about the nursery. Damn it. This is yet another sign that I shouldn't be the sales manager of the distillery. Maybe I should consider another career. I can't be a pro surfer but there must be a job that doesn't involve me sitting behind a desk eight hours a day.

I elbow Kai. "You're just happy about this because you want to get Harper pregnant."

I'm teasing, but guessing by the smile on his face, he is trying to get Harper pregnant.

"I promised to give Harper a family. And whatever my fiancée wants, she gets."

"Smuggler's Hideaway won't know what hit it when the Raider brothers all have children in school."

Eli chuckles as he joins us. "Why do you think I paid to have the jail cells refurbished?"

I point to Kai. "Because he's a troublemaker."

He chuckles. "Says the man who got caught crowing like a rooster naked at four in the morning outside the gates of *Mermaid Mystical Gardens.*"

"It was a bet," I say as if a bet can excuse any behavior. Because it can.

"At least he was outside the gates," Eli says. "He avoided a burglary charge."

I was outside because I couldn't figure out a way to sneak into the amusement park without scaling the gates, which wasn't happening, considering I was naked.

"Come on." Eli nudges me toward the nursery. "Go check out the room. Who knows? Maybe you'll have need of its services soon."

I scowl. I won't be needing a nursery anytime soon.

I step into the room and nearly stumble at the vision before me. There are three cribs. One each for Stephanie, Mira, and Adele. The walls are painted an ocean blue with illustrations of mermaids, mermen, and other mythical sea creatures. There's a rocking chair in one corner. A bookcase filled with books in another. And baskets of toys lined up along the wall.

"How much did this cost?" I mutter.

Eli pats my arm. "You keep selling the booze and money won't be an issue."

"Yeah, yeah. I know."

"I'm sorry you injured your shoulder again, but the surfing world's loss is our gain. You'll have more time to work at the distillery until you're healed."

The surfing world's loss. The surfing world has forgotten I existed. My time on the pro tour doesn't even qualify as a one-day wonder.

And now I'm stuck selling liquor for my family's distillery. My dreams have all come true.

Chapter 8

Someday I'm going to stop allowing Dad's words to hurt me. Today is not that day.

Hazel

"I'm here!" I shout as I enter the Harris family farmhouse.

"We're in the kitchen."

I nearly groan at Mom's answer. Of course, she's in the kitchen. Dad is a big believer in dividing up chores based on gender. Women do all the work inside the house. Men do the farming and repair work on the exterior of the house.

When I enter the kitchen, Mom is removing a tray from the oven while Sadie chops up vegetables and Scarlett peels potatoes.

"Where are Thomas and Ian?" I ask because I will never stop poking at the gender roles my parents believe in.

Mom frowns. "They're in the basement watching football with your dad and Weston."

"Why do they get to relax when we have to cook?" Told you I can't stop poking at my parents.

"Hazel," Sadie mutters.

"What? Would you prefer to discuss your pen pal?"

It's a good thing those lasers in her eyes aren't real because I would be burned to a crisp if they were. Someone wants to keep her affair with a soldier a secret. Ha! As if it's possible to keep a secret on this island.

"Shut up," she grits out.

"Girls!" Mom yells. "Behave. Can't we have one Sunday dinner without a fight?"

Weston chuckles as he enters the kitchen. "If I know one thing about sisters, it's how much they love to fight."

Scarlett rolls her eyes. "You only have one sister."

"And you've met Sophia. You know how much she loves to fight."

Scarlett pushes up on her toes to kiss his cheek. "Only with you."

He lifts an eyebrow. "Have you not met her best friends, Chloe, Nova, Maya, and Paisley? Those five are always fighting about something. How they haven't burned down their brewery yet is a mystery."

I snort. "As if Paisley would allow anything to happen to her precious brewery."

Paisley's the master brewer of *Five Fathoms Brewing*. She's also uptight about the brewing facilities. When a hurricane hit the island a while back and ruined the brewery, she nearly lost her mind. Until her archnemesis, Eli, stepped in. Now they're in love and have a baby girl.

"I forgot Paisley and you are bosom buddies since she's engaged to Miles's brother."

I scowl at Weston. "I don't have anything to do with Miles."

He opens his mouth but I slam my hand over it before he can speak. He's not telling the entire world about New Year's Eve. Although, guessing by how Scarlett is smirking, he already told her.

He peels my fingers away before sauntering to the refrigerator and pulling out a beer. "Anyone else want one?"

"Yes, please."

Mom's lips purse at my response. Women shouldn't drink beer is another one of her mantras. She should give up, considering I am never going to follow her rules.

I keep my eyes locked on her as I take a nice, long sip of my beer. She huffs before returning her attention to the stove to stir a pot of gravy.

Ian and Thomas rush into the kitchen but screech to a halt when they notice Weston helping Scarlett with the potatoes.

"What are you doing up here helping?" Ian asks.

"You were supposed to bring us beers," Thomas adds.

Weston motions to the refrigerator. "Help yourself."

"Or do you need me to show you how to open the door?"

Thomas scowls at me. "Don't be a brat."

I bat my eyelashes. "I'm the brat? I'm not the one who was lazing on a chair watching television while the rest of his family works in the kitchen."

He shrugs. "Dad and Ian aren't helping either."

"Not helping your case," Weston mutters.

"Let it go," Mom insists.

"Why should I? Do you realize what century we live in? It's ridiculous to expect women to do all the cooking and cleaning while the men sit around watching television and farting and scratching their balls."

She gasps. "Hazel Edith!"

"Someone got the middle name treatment," Ian sings.

Guess what? I get the middle name treatment a lot. When I was younger, I tried to keep my middle name a secret. Who wants to be called Edith these days? But it was impossible considering Mom's tendency to give me the middle name treatment.

Dad strolls into the kitchen. "I hear complaining. Hazel must be here."

"I wasn't complaining. I was pointing out the inequality of gender roles during Sunday family meals."

Thomas groans. "Here we go again. Does the feminist need her soapbox?"

"What I need is to get out of this kitchen."

Ian sighs. "I don't know why you're bitching. It's not as if you're never in the kitchen. Especially since you're still working at *Smuggler's Cove Restaurant*."

Dad grunts. "No daughter of mine should be working at a restaurant."

I throw my arms in the air. "Where else am I going to work? There aren't enough people on this island for me to work full-time as a therapist."

"I told you the physical therapy degree was a waste of time."

Scarlett squeezes my hand but I shake her off. We are not the same. While I stayed on the island and pushed back against our parents, Scarlett escaped for a decade. She nearly didn't stay, even after she fell in love with Weston. Dad has no idea how hard he is on us girls.

"Disagree. What I do helps people. For example, I helped Caleb learn to walk again without a limp."

Dad scowls. "You said it yourself. You don't have enough therapy work."

"First of all, thank you for acknowledging what an awesome job I did with Caleb. I'm pretty proud of it."

Mom clears her throat. "Hazel."

"What? Am I not allowed to be proud of my work?" I ask even though I know exactly why she's scolding me.

I'm not allowed to toot my own horn. And I'm definitely not allowed to sass Dad. Two things I do often. And well if I do say so myself. And there I go tooting my own horn again. I guess it's a habit.

"You should find a good man to marry."

I groan. "I'm not letting a man solve my problems, Dad. I can solve them myself."

"You can?" He lifts an eyebrow. "You're twenty-seven and still working at a restaurant."

"First of all, there's nothing wrong with working at *Smuggler's Cove Restaurant*. I have flexible hours, and the tips are amazing." Dad opens his mouth to respond. "And, secondly, maybe I'll stop working there when I find another job," I blurt out before he can speak.

"Another job?" Sadie asks. "You didn't mention you were looking for another job."

Because I'm not. I only said I was to stop Dad from making another derogatory comment about my life.

"But you also said there aren't enough people for you to work full-time as a physical therapist here."

Which is why it might be time for me to consider moving away from the island. I love my home. And I love my family – no matter how much Dad and Mom tick me off. But maybe it's time to explore other possibilities.

I wink at Sadie. "There are more places in the world than Smuggler's Hideaway. You know, places where soldiers are sent to defend our country."

"What soldier?" Dad asks and Sadie's shoulders sag with relief. The rumors about her pen pal have not reached his ears. She's not ready to tell our parents about Ben. She better get ready because the rumors will reach Mom and Dad eventually. "Are you considering enlisting in the military? No daughter of mine will enlist."

"Technically, I wouldn't enlist. I'd be commissioned as an officer."

I did my internship at an Army Medical Retention Processing Unit. Before I finished the internship, the commander pulled me aside and basically promised me whatever I wanted if I joined the Army. Except she couldn't promise me a duty station near Smuggler's Hideaway, which was the one condition I insisted on.

Weston wraps an arm around Scarlett's shoulders and pulls her near. "We should get out of firing range."

Dad slams a fist on the countertop. "I don't care if you're a sergeant or a captain. No daughter of mine is joining the military."

"I'm confused—"

"Hazel," Sadie interrupts. "Stop egging him on. You're going to give him a heart attack and I have a shift at the motel this afternoon. I can't be spending my evening at the hospital."

"Fine. But only because you asked nicely. I'm not considering joining the Army. But I am searching for a therapist position on the Mainland."

I haven't exactly started searching yet, but I probably should. I can't keep going the way I am now. Scrambling together enough money each month for rent on my apartment and my practice. Listening to Dad complain about my job at the restaurant at every family meal. Watching YouTube videos to repair my therapy equipment since I can't afford to update any of it.

Besides, if I leave the island, I won't have to treat Miles. Or see him and his bright blue eyes anymore. Or touch his muscular chest. Or give in to him again.

Huh. This leaving the island idea is becoming more and more appealing by the minute.

Chapter 9

Things are changing. Starting now.

Miles

I whistle as I enter Hazel's physical therapy practice. I've been looking forward to seeing Hazel since our last session. Although, I could do without the torture.

"Hello!" I call out when Hazel doesn't appear. I know she's not treating another patient since all the doors are open.

"Come on in," she hollers from the treatment room.

I frown. No sarcastic response? I make my way into the room.

"Good morning, Bl—." I clear my throat. "Hazel."

She smiles, but her green eyes don't sparkle.

"What's wrong?"

She motions to the treatment table. "Hop on. We'll start with some stretching exercises to combat stiffness and improve flexibility."

I don't move. "No."

Her brow wrinkles. "Sorry, Miles. I know you're in a hurry to get back on your surfboard, but I don't think you're ready for pendulum swings or pulley-assisted stretches yet."

"I'm not in a hurry."

"You're not?"

"Nope."

Because the longer I'm injured, the more time I can spend with Hazel.

"Okay." She pats the treatment table. "Let's get to work on those stretches then."

"No."

"I am not in the mood for your riddles today, Miles."

Now we're getting somewhere.

"You're always in the mood for my riddles. What's going on?"

"I'm fine and it's none of your business."

"You're not fine, and we're not starting therapy until you tell me what's wrong."

She fists her hands on her hips. Finally, she's showing a bit of life. "Did you forget the part about it being none of your business?"

"Wrong."

"Miles." She growls. "We aren't together anymore. We're not even friends. My life is not your business."

"We are friends," I grit out. "Something's wrong with you and I'm not letting you put your hands on my injured shoulder when you're obviously upset."

"I'm not upset."

"And you don't have that little wrinkle on your forehead you always get when you're upset."

She slaps her forehead. "I don't get a wrinkle on my forehead when I'm upset."

"Yes, you do." I step closer until I'm crowding her. This room is small and she has nowhere to go. "When Scarlett moved off the island, you got the wrinkle. When Ian fell off the tractor and broke his leg and arm, you got the wrinkle. When—"

She holds up a hand. "Stop. I don't need a history lesson on all the times I've been upset in my life."

I grasp her hand. Electricity tingles where our skin touches but I ignore it. This moment isn't about us. It's about Hazel. No matter what she may think of me, I will never allow her to suffer. Not if I can help it.

"How can I help?"

"Help? You want to help me?"

"Of course. I care about you." I massage my thumb into her wrist. Her eyes darken until they're nearly emerald. It's the same color they turn when I bury myself deep inside her. My cock twitches at the reminder.

She yanks her hand away. "You don't care about me. I'm your past and you're feeling nostalgic is all."

I'm not arguing with her about whether I care about her or not. I know how I feel.

"Are we doing this therapy session or not?"

"Not until you tell me what's wrong."

"You're like a dog with a bone."

"Woof! Woof!"

She drops her chin to her chest, but not before I notice her smile.

"Fine. We had a Sunday family meal at the farmhouse yesterday, and Dad got all over my case for working at the restaurant, and now I have to find a job and move off the island."

My heart lodges in my throat. Off the island? She's moving? She's abandoning me? Not if I can help it.

"Slow down. Explain yourself. Your dad got all over your case?"

She scowls. "You know what he thinks of women. They should stay in the kitchen. And get married to a farmer."

"I thought he eased up after the Christmas before last when Scarlett nearly left Weston because she didn't want to live on Smuggler's Hideaway."

Her eyes narrow on me. "How do you know what happened with Scarlett and my dad?"

I shrug. "You grew up on this island. You know how everyone loves to gossip."

"Whatever," she grumbles. "Dad eased up on Scarlett, but he hasn't eased up on me. He thinks I should get married and that my therapy degree was a waste of time."

"Your therapy degree wasn't a waste of time. You help people to heal. It's important."

"That's what I said."

"And?"

"And then I got mad he didn't acknowledge how important my work is and told everyone I was looking for a job off the island."

Relief fills me. She's not going anywhere. She spoke out in anger.

"And now I have to find a job on the mainland."

"No, you don't. The argument with your dad will be forgotten by the next time you see him."

Hazel and her dad were always arguing in high school. I witnessed several of their shouting matches in the farmhouse. No matter how loud they shouted at each other, her dad never let her down. He showed up at every single one of her basketball matches. He picked her up from parties when she'd had too much moonshine to drink.

I would have loved to have him as a dad. My dad abandoned our family when I was twelve. I never felt his loss, though. Eli and Rhett stepped up. Eli worked multiple jobs to help Mom out financially while Rhett took us to school and all of our sports activities and made sure we finished our homework.

"It doesn't matter what Dad thinks. It's time for me to leave."

My heart stutters in my chest. She can't leave. I won't let her. "Why?"

"Why what?"

"Why is it time for you to leave? You love this island."

"Love it or not, I don't have enough work for my practice. And I'm tired of working at the restaurant."

"There are other jobs you can do on the side."

"I don't want to do side gigs. I want to work full-time in the career I spent six years of my life studying for. I want to help people. I don't want to serve drinks to tourists or work at the amusement park or any of the other tourist traps."

Shit. She's thought this through. This isn't a spur of the moment decision.

"You're serious? You'd move away from Smuggler's Hideaway?"

"I prefer not to. I'll research if any of the towns on the Mainland within an hour's drive have any openings first. But if not..." She trails off with a shrug.

"I never thought you'd leave the island."

"Never say never," she sings before motioning to the table. "You figured out what's bugging me. No more excuses."

I whip off my shirt before laying on the table. "Have you started your job search yet?"

"I've done some searching online. I found an interesting position about two hours away. Two hours is too far to commute, so I'd have to move."

She can't move. I can't let her go. I always thought Hazel would be here waiting for me. But she's not waiting. She's moving on with her life.

It's me who's been waiting. I've been waiting to be ready to settle down. To untangle the mess in my head. To figure out where I belong.

I still don't know where I belong but I know one thing with absolute certainty. I can't let Hazel move away. I need to win her back. I need to convince her I'm worthy of a second chance.

Because I've always loved this woman. I've just been too chicken shit to try and win her back. Too worried she'd make a fool out of me.

I'm done caring about how foolish I'll look. Or how much she'll make me work for a second chance.

Hazel is mine and I won't stop until she realizes the truth. We belong together.

Chapter 10

Cheating is in the eye of the beholder.

Hazel

I drum my fingers on the steering wheel as I sit in my car in the parking lot of *Sirens & Saddles.* I'm not ready for another family event. Not after the previous Sunday dinner ended with me searching for a job off the island.

I scan the parking lot for Dad's car but don't find it. Of course, the family farm isn't too far away. Mom and Dad could easily walk here.

Shoot a smuggler. I'm out of excuses.

I search for my family as I walk toward the entrance but no one's here. I check my watch. I'm five minutes late. They should be here bitching about my tardiness.

"Hazel!" Warren hollers as he approaches.

Warren is the son of the owner of the horse stables. He's also an entitled bully who thinks that because he's going to inherit this business, he can say and do whatever he wants. In other words, he's an asshole.

"Warren." I nod to him.

"I'm glad you agreed to today's date."

Today's date? I never agreed to a date. Let alone one with an entitled bully.

"What are you talking about?"

He grins. "Today's date. You and me. Out on the horses exploring the riding trails around the island. I had my assistant pack us a picnic." He waggles his eyebrows. "It'll be romantic."

I hold up my finger. "I need to make one phone call."

I don't wait for his response before marching away. I find a secluded spot and ring Scarlett.

"Hi, Ha—"

I don't let her finish her greeting. "What in the name of mermaids in the sea is going on?"

She sighs. "I told Dad you'd be mad."

"There was a family discussion about setting me up with Warren the bully for a date?"

"Don't get your panties in a twist. When you messaged me to say you'd see me today, I phoned Mom because I hadn't received an invitation for a family day."

"Because there is no family day. It's a set-up."

"It's a set-up."

"I can't believe this. You were right to escape the island for a decade."

"You're still thinking about leaving?"

"Started sending in applications yesterday."

After talking everything over with Miles, I knew it was time. I can't keep living the way I'm living. I'm twenty-seven and thirty is approaching fast. I shouldn't be living paycheck to paycheck. I want to follow my dream of being a therapist. Something I can't do on this island.

I called around to therapy practices in the closest towns on the Mainland. Unfortunately, no one had a vacant position. Which led me to the internet and some vacancies a bit further away.

Scarlett mumbles something but I don't understand.

"Did you swear at me in Japanese?"

Scarlett is a Japanese translator.

"I didn't swear at you. I'm going to miss you. I haven't been back on the island long and now you're leaving."

"Yeah, well, staying doesn't seem viable when Mom and Dad are setting me up on dates with assholes."

"You could get back together with Miles."

"And you could find yourself waking up in bed to a clown staring down at you at four in the morning."

"Weston would shoot you."

"Not if I stole his service weapon first."

"He keeps it locked in a safe."

"His safe opens with his thumbprint."

She groans. "Please tell me you don't have my fiancé's thumbprint."

"I admit to nothing."

"Hey, Hazel!" Warren shouts from behind me and now it's my turn to groan. "We need to get going."

I wave at him. "Be right there."

"Don't do it," Scarlett orders.

I inject my voice with as much innocence as possible. "Do what?"

"If you leave now, Dad will just keep trying."

"He'll keep trying anyway."

"Not if you tell him about your job search."

I groan. "No, then he'll bitch about me leaving."

"You love horseback riding. Go have fun with the horses and forget all about this being a date."

Warren marches toward me.

"Easier said than done," I mutter before hanging up on Scarlett.

"Sorry." I shove my phone in my back pocket. "I needed to reassure a patient."

"A patient?" He snorts. "You're a physical therapist. Not a doctor."

Oh, goodie, the obnoxiousness has begun.

"Where are our horses?" I walk toward the stables without waiting for his answer. I'm being rude, but it's better than slamming my fist in his crooked nose. Although, a broken nose might fix it. Something to think about.

We reach the stables and I allow Warren to lead me to a stall. "This is Ginger. I thought you'd want to ride her since you're a ginger."

"Very observant. I do have red hair."

He wiggles his eyebrows. "Do the carpets match the drapes?"

I fist my hands before I punch him. Why are my parents obsessed with this jerk? I'm not the only sister they've set up with him. Sadie has also been a victim of their matchmaking. But she's smarter than me. She faked a stomach bug and made retching noises in the restroom until Warren left.

"I don't like carpets," I say and watch as Warren tries not to swallow his tongue.

While he's frozen in place, I open the stall and lead Ginger out. "Aren't you a pretty girl?"

A saddle pad and saddle are already on her back. I quickly check she's comfortable with the equipment before leading her out of the stables.

"You ready to go?" I ask Warren before mounting the horse. "Which trail?"

I'd ride off without him but I didn't check which trails are safe – trails can get flooded or overrun by sand dunes – before I arrived. Because I thought this was a fun family day.

Warren mounts his horse and joins me before answering. "The Tipsy Trail."

I frown at Warren's answer. The Tipsy Trail is a gentle ride for beginners or bachelorette party groups who drink too much moonshine.

"What about Rumrunner's Ridge?" It's a steep, winding trail the Prohibitionists supposedly used to hide the good stuff.

"Ginger's not good with steep trails."

"What about Whiskey Creek Run?"

"Hazel." He scowls at me. "I'm the expert here and I have decided we're riding the Tipsy Trail."

I roll my eyes. If he was such an expert, he'd know I've been riding horses since I was five and can handle all of the difficult trails, including Bootlegger's Bend that twists like a drunken sailor's story.

"I'll lead," he says as he clicks his tongue and his horse begins prancing toward the start of the trail.

I glare at his back. At least if he leads, he can't stare at my ass the entire time.

We ride for a few minutes before we reach the beach. Warren slows down until I'm next to him.

"How have you been, Hazel? We haven't spoken for a while."

"I'm fine."

"Your dad said you're still working at the *Smuggler's Cove Restaurant*. You're kind of old to be a waitress."

Wow. Isn't he full of compliments?

"I'm the hostess, and it's part-time."

"Part-time? Must be nice not to have to work full-time."

Must be nice to have a daddy who owns a business where he can fart around all day and say he works full-time when everyone on the island knows he doesn't work past three every day.

"I also have my therapy practice."

"I thought the therapy practice was a hobby."

I inhale a deep breath through my nose before I snap at him. A hobby? I spent six years at college for a hobby?

"Not a hobby," I manage to mutter. "Actually, I'm searching for a new job."

"We have an open position here. It's part-time. It's perfect for a woman who's planning to start a family soon." He winks and I nearly gag.

"I'm not planning on starting a family anytime soon."

"You might change your mind if the right man comes along."

"I don't have time for a man now. I need to find a new job *as a therapist.* And then I'll be busy concentrating on growing my practice and career."

"This is the problem with women nowadays. They're always worried about their careers when they should be busy having children and maintaining families."

Wow. I knew Warren was a jerk. I didn't realize he was a sexist jerk. Good to know.

"Where's our picnic?"

"Shellshock Canyon."

"Shellshock Canyon is at the bottom of Cannonball Hill. We can use Pirate's Shortcut to get to Cannonball Hill."

"Cannonball Hill is dangerous."

"It'll be fine." I reach down to pat Ginger's neck. "Ginger and I are looking forward to the challenge."

"Pirate's Shortcut will take twice as long to get to Shellshock Canyon than if we stay on the Tipsy Trail."

"Not if we race."

"Racing wouldn't be fair. I'll beat you by a mile."

I smirk. "Oh yeah? Sounds like a challenge."

"I'm not..."

I don't listen to him. I squeeze Ginger's sides with my calves while commanding her to 'hup'. She gallops away, leaving Warren in our wake.

I hear him behind us commanding his horse to hurry up but I don't turn around. I intend to win this race and show this pompous, sexist, nepo baby women are as good as – if not better – than men.

Pirate's Shortcut isn't exactly a shortcut but lucky for me, I do know of a shortcut to get to Cannonball Hill. I make a sharp left at Hidden Keg Hollow and cross the path of the Tipsy Trail before reaching the top of the hill.

"You sure about this, girl?" I ask Ginger. She doesn't hesitate. She gallops down the hill as if possessed. My hair flies behind me, my heart pounds in my chest, and the smile on my face stretches from ear to ear.

This is why I love this island. I doubt you'll find bridal paths as wild and crazy as these anywhere else in the country.

I pat Ginger's neck and slow her down as we reach Shell-shock Canyon.

"You cheated!" Warren shouts as he catches up to us.

"How did I cheat?"

"You didn't stay on Pirate's Shortcut."

I shrug. "I never said I would."

"You're a cheater. No wonder you haven't found a man."

I groan. "You haven't found a woman either."

"I am a man. I need to sow my wild oats first."

I already sowed my wild oats. I didn't realize what I was doing at the time. I thought I had found the man of my dreams. The man I'd build a family with.

Miles proved me wrong.

Chapter 11

Step one. Convince Hazel she doesn't hate me.

MILES

"Come on." I try herding my family into *Smuggler's Cove Restaurant.*

"What's your hurry?" Zane asks as he bounces Adele in his arms.

"It's the Smuggler's Reenactment Dinner. I want good seats."

Sloane snorts. "Sure, good seats. You aren't rushing us because Hazel's working tonight."

I haven't seen Hazel since our last therapy session. I want to check on her. Make sure she's okay.

Especially since I heard a rumor about her getting set up on a date with Warren. He was a bully in high school who thought it was funny to tease the girls when they were on their periods. He better not have upset my Blaze.

Kai smirks. "Excellent. We can spend the entire night watching Miles crash and burn."

"There better not be any food burning," Henry grumbles. "I'm starving."

"Dad." Harper wags her finger at him. "No unhealthy food for you."

He throws his arms in the air. "What's the point of living if I can't eat unhealthy food?"

"The point is being alive."

"Don't push it, young lady. It's bad enough I'm in this damn wheelchair."

"But if you weren't in the wheelchair, I couldn't do this." Kai races down the sidewalk while pushing Henry, who whoops with joy as Kai pops a wheelie.

Harper groans. "Now I have two people to care for."

I scowl. This family is more difficult to control than a herd of sheep that discovered an opening in the fence leading to an apple orchard. Who knew sheep go crazy for apples?

Mom pats my arm. "Let's go ahead, dear. They'll follow."

My step-dad, Stuart, opens the door for us and I escort Mom inside. Hazel looks up from her hostess station and smiles at us. The breath whooshes out of me. There's nothing better than watching her pouty, pink mouth smile at me.

Mere weeks ago, she scowled whenever she saw me. But now, after a couple of therapy sessions during which we talked, she's smiling at me.

"Uh oh. I was hoping the reservation for the Raider bunch was a mistake." Hazel winks.

I wiggle my eyebrows. "Don't think you can handle us?"

She snorts. "I can handle you, but I don't have to. Once your butts are in seats, you're the waitress's problem."

"Not all of our butts are here." I motion outside to where Kai is giving Pearl, Rhett, and Dakota's oldest girl a ride in a wheelchair while Zane encourages him and Rhett glowers. "Don't suppose you can help me wrangle the Raider bunch?"

She raises her eyebrow. "Is this a challenge?"

I forgot how much my girl loves challenges. I nod. "Yes, it is."

"Be right back." She marches to the door and flings it open. "Hey, Raider bunch! Get your butts inside or I'll tell the chef you're all on a liquid diet and can only eat porridge tonight."

Kai freezes. "No steak? No cranberry cheesecake?"

"Not unless your butt is in your seat at your table within the next minute."

Rhett snags Pearl from the wheelchair. "Let's go. I've been looking forward to the Hasselback potatoes all week."

The Raider crew bustles inside and aims straight for the large table in the corner. No one argues about who is sitting where – a favorite Raider pastime – and everyone is seated within a minute. It's a smuggler miracle.

"Challenge complete," Hazel says as she sets a menu down in front of me.

"Someone has a crush," Kai sings.

I glare at him. "Don't embarrass Hazel."

"Dude." Zane snorts. "Hazel is long gone. He's referring to your blush."

I scowl. "I don't blush."

"What's a crush?" Pearl asks.

"Remember when you liked that boy at school, Harold?" Dakota asks and Pearl nods. "That's a crush."

"Uncle Miles! Do you have a crush on Hazel?" Pearl shouts.

"No." My feelings for Hazel are way more than a crush.

"But she's pretty. You should marry her."

Maybe I will. But first, I need Hazel to give me a second chance.

"What about this Harold guy? Do you intend to marry him?"

Her nose wrinkles. "Gross. I'm five."

"And you shouldn't be interested in boys," Rhett growls.

Zane and Eli nod in agreement.

"Save me from girl dads," Paisley mutters as she tweaks Stephanie's nose.

Jaxon frowns as he scans the table. "This is very odd."

"What's odd, nerd boy?" Blossom asks.

He motions to the table. "All of the grandchildren are girls."

"Do you not like girls?"

"I think I've proven how much I like girls," he mutters and Blossom's breath hitches. I never expected their fake marriage to become real, but it's obvious how much those two love each other.

My stomach clenches. I want what they have. A woman who loves me. A woman who looks at me as if I hang the moon every night.

I glance over my shoulder. Hazel is greeting a new group at the front of the restaurant. And there's the woman I want it all with. She notices me and smiles. My jealousy fades away. There's no reason to be jealous when I will have a woman who loves me in my arms soon.

Jaxon pushes his glasses up his nose. "I'm merely wondering what the probability is of the six sons of a man who could only create boys, only creating girls."

"Huh." Paisley taps her chin. "This is interesting. We should calculate the odds."

Eli wraps his arm around her shoulders and hauls her close to kiss her temple. "You're not doing any calculations while we're having a family dinner."

The door flies open and bangs against the wall. Two men dressed as smugglers rush inside.

Pearl claps. "It's starting!"

"We need to hide," the first smuggler says.

The second smuggler glances around the room. "We need to hurry. The Prohis will be here soon."

"We should have used the tunnels under City Hall. The Prohis wouldn't follow us there."

"I told you the tunnels are flooded."

A whistle blows outside and the smugglers rush forward. "Let's hide under the empty table over there."

They've barely managed to crawl under the table when the door opens and two men dressed as Prohibition agents enter.

"Where are they?" The Prohi points his billy club at a woman diner.

"Can you be more specific? Where are who?"

He growls as he swaggers toward her. "Don't make me arrest you for interfering with police business?"

Pearl climbs onto her chair. "I know where they are!"

Rhett wraps an arm around her thighs to steady her. "You're supposed to pretend you don't."

"Is it a game?"

"Yes, it's a game."

"I love games." Pearl giggles. "They went into the kitchen!"

The Prohibition agents saunter our way. "Are you certain, little lady?"

"Yep. They went that way." She points to the kitchen.

"If you're wrong, we'll arrest you."

She fists her hands at her hips. "No, you won't. Daddy will protect me."

Rhett nods and pulls her into his arms. No one is messing with his daughter.

"All right, little lady." The Prohibition agents rush to the kitchen.

"You can come out now!" Pearl shouts once they're gone.

The smugglers climb out from under the table. "Thanks, miss." They tip their hats to her before scurrying out of the restaurant.

Applause breaks out.

"That's it?" a man yells. "I paid one-hundred dollars per plate for that?"

Hazel rushes to him. "Don't worry, sir. The show isn't over."

"It barely began."

He stands to get in her face and I spring to my feet. I position myself in front of Hazel to shield her. "Do not yell at her."

Hazel tries to push in front of me. "This is my job. I don't need you to save me."

"I know, Blaze. But I'm not going to sit there while some guy is an asshole to you."

She snorts. "What? The role of being an asshole to Hazel is reserved exclusively for you?"

I palm her cheek. "I'm not an asshole to you."

She cocks an eyebrow.

"Not anymore."

"Hello! Did you forget I exist?" The man thumps a fist on the table.

I growl at him. "You're done."

"Done?"

"Get your shit. Your evening is over."

"I want a refund."

I dig my wallet out and remove a few fifty-dollar bills. "Here. Consider this your refund."

The man snatches the money. "I'm writing a bad review," he grumbles as he marches away.

His dinner companion sighs as she stands. "Don't worry. He's too lazy to write a review."

"You're free to stay," Hazel shouts after her.

The woman waves in response.

Hazel's shoulders fall. "I hope he's nicer to her than he was to me."

I tuck a strand of hair behind her ear. “You can’t save everyone, Blaze.”

She scowls. “I told you. We’re not together anymore. I’m not Blaze. You may refer to me as Hazel.”

She doesn’t wait for my response before marching away. She’s glorious with her red hair flying behind her.

We’re not together yet, Blaze. But it will happen. And then I’m never letting you go.

Chapter 12

This is why I don't enjoy karaoke.

HAZEL

"Let's go!" Sadie pushes me toward the bar.

"I'm tired. I don't need a night out. I need a night of sleep." Searching for a new job on top of working two jobs is exhausting.

"Too bad," Scarlett says. "If you're leaving this island, we need to get as many sisters' nights in as we can."

I groan. "Have you been practicing giving guilt trips?"

She beams at me. "I have. What did you think?"

I give her a thumbs-up. "Good job. Your children will always do what you say. They'll resent the hell out of you, but they'll follow your orders."

"Nope. I'll bring them with me on work trips to Japan. They'll love me and probably be bilingual before they start kindergarten."

"Why don't you take me on trips to Japan with you?" Sadie asks. "I'm a great traveling companion."

I giggle. "A great traveling companion? You have to pee every half-hour and are very particular about where you're willing to go."

Her nose wrinkles. "I wasn't peeing behind a tree. We were less than five feet from the highway."

"Who cares? No one wants to watch you pee."

"Ha! Remember the car honking at you when you dropped your pants to pee." She curls her lip. "No strangers are honking at me while I've got my pants around my ankles."

"You could at least not drink a can of soda every hour."

"We weren't allowed soda unless we were on a road trip. I wasn't missing out."

"Sisters." Scarlett claps her hands. "Can we forget about stuff that happened over a decade ago and go have some fun?"

"Yep." Sadie skips to the door. She opens it and motions me inside.

I groan. "Do we have to go to karaoke?"

"Count your blessings. It's not Mermaid Karaoke."

Mermaid Karaoke sounds made up, but it's an actual thing. In the summer, Smuggler's Hideaway is inundated with tourists. The women dress up as mermaids and sing karaoke at the *Bootlegger* bar in the hopes of capturing a smuggler. The men buy them shots of moonshine and it's a party.

I step inside the bar with my sisters and allow my eyes to adjust to the dim light. The music starts up and a dramatic piano chord plays. Addy jumps on stage and grabs the microphone. She begins singing *I Will Survive* while dancing around the stage.

"Uh oh. Who broke Addy's heart?" I ask.

"I don't care," Sadie says. "Girl can sing."

It's true. Addy can sing. She's wasted working as a waitress at *Five Fathoms Brewing*.

We make our way through the crowd to a table at the side of the stage. The bar is packed with locals enjoying a Friday night out. Once tourist season hits, no one will have time for a night out since most people work at least two jobs in the summer.

We barely have a chance to sit down before the bartender, Alaia, arrives. She sets a bottle of moonshine on the table along with three shot glasses.

"We didn't order this."

She nods behind her. I crane my neck to see who she's nodding at. I scowl before getting to my feet and stomping across the bar.

"What the hell, Miles?"

He frowns. "What?"

I poke his chest. Bad idea. I can feel his hard muscles. Muscles I've touched a thousand times with my hands and my tongue. Concentrate, Hazel!

"Dude, you can't get me drunk because you want in my pants!"

His face pales. "Shit. I'm not trying to get you drunk. I'm treating you and your sisters to a drink."

"If you want to treat us, order us some Smuggler's Martinis. Not a bottle of moonshine."

"You're right. I apologize. Three Smuggler's Martinis coming right up."

To my surprise, Miles rushes to our table and nabs the bottle of moonshine before making his way to the bar. I return to the table where Scarlett and Sadie are sitting with their mouths gaping open.

"What?"

"You refused free moonshine." Sadie reaches across the table to place her hand on my forehead. I slap her hand away.

"We're getting Smuggler's Martinis instead."

"I haven't had a Smuggler's Martini in forever," Scarlett says.

Alaia returns carrying a tray filled with martinis. "Three Smuggler's Martinis for the Harris women." She hands out the drinks and tucks the tray under her arm. "Remember. These look innocent but pack a serious punch – just like a true Smuggler."

Sadie raises her glass in the air. "Smuggler's Martinis. Perfect for people who enjoy their secrets shaken, not stirred."

I sip on my drink and nearly choke. I forgot how potent these drinks are. Two shots of moonshine and one shot of coconut rum is no joke.

"What secrets are you shaking and not stirring?" Scarlett asks Sadie.

"None," Sadie squeaks. "We're next."

She stands and grasps my hand. I try to tug my hand free but she holds strong. "I'm not singing."

"You have to. It's our turn."

"I'll sing if Scarlett does."

Scarlett hates singing in front of crowds. But, to my surprise, she sets her drink down and stands. "What song are we singing?"

Sadie raises a fist in the air. "Yes! The Harris girls are on fire tonight."

The music begins and I groan when I hear the bright, sparkly synth glissando, followed by energetic and fizzy synths designed to create a feeling of excitement.

"I am not singing 'Girls Just Want to Have Fun'!" I shout at Sadie.

She slaps a microphone in my hand. "Yes, you are."

I retreat toward the back of the stage but Scarlett grabs my arm and pulls me to the front. "I'm not doing this alone."

"We wouldn't have to do this at all if you didn't stand up!"

"What fun is sitting in the corner? Are you a smuggler or not?"

I glare at her. Did she forget I can't back away from a challenge? She smirks. She didn't forget.

The lyrics are displayed at the bottom of the monitor and I begin to sing. I scan the crowd. Everyone in here is going to be talking about how bad the Harris girls are at singing tomorrow.

I spot Miles and he gives me a thumbs-up as he maneuvers toward the front of the stage. He dances to the music as he mouths the lyrics. He looks ridiculous. I can't help but laugh.

"Hazel! Hazel! Hazel!" he chants as he raises his phone in the air with a picture of a flame on it. He sways from side to side as he switches from chanting to singing and back again.

"Holy mermaids. Stop!" I shout but Sadie elbows me and points to the lyrics. Ugh. This is why I don't do karaoke.

The song finally ends and Miles breaks into applause while whistling. "The Harris girls have got it going on!"

"You're ridiculous."

"But I'm not wrong."

Sadie bows. "Thank you."

I roll my eyes and push my sisters off the stage. "I am never doing karaoke with you again."

"I don't know why not. It was fun. Plus," Scarlett points to our table, "fresh Smuggler's Martinis have appeared."

"Yum!" Sadie grabs a glass and drinks half of the martini in one go.

"I am not holding your hair back when you puke."

She points to her ponytail. "No need. I came prepared."

Scarlett sways in her seat. "Weston is going to be annoyed when I message him to pick me up because I'm too drunk to drive."

"Oh, please." I roll my eyes. "Weston is probably planning on invading our girls' night out anyway."

"He can't. He's not a girl. I know. I have proof."

Sadie leans in close. "Do you have pictures?"

Scarlett rears back, and her chair wobbles. I grab the armrest before she falls over. "Someone's not used to *Buccaneer's Moonshine* anymore."

"My sister asked for a picture of my boyfriend's private parts. I'm allowed to be shocked."

"Private parts?" Sadie barks out a laugh. "What are you? Fifty? No one our age says private parts."

"Did you forget when my birthday is?" Scarlett narrows her eyes at Sadie but the action makes her sway again.

"I should get you some coffee."

"Oh, goodie. I'll have an espresso martini."

"Me too!" Sadie shouts.

I wag my finger at her. "No way. The last time you drank espresso martinis, you thought you were completely sober and decided to cut your own hair. You cried for hours the next day when you woke up with the scissors in your hand, surrounded by mounds of hair."

"Fine." She huffs. "A shot of moonshine and a beer, please."

"I—"

My answer is cut off when the music begins. A slow, repeating arpeggiated chord progression establishes a romantic and gentle atmosphere. I glance at the stage. Miles is standing with the microphone in his hand.

Oh no. Is Miles going to sing the most romantic song in the world – aka *Perfect* by Ed Sheeran – at karaoke?

"Oh my mermaid, Miles is singing a sappy love song to all the smugglers in *Bootlegger*."

"Nope." Scarlett shakes her head and nearly falls over again. "Miles Raider is singing a sappy love song to you."

"He is not."

She points to Miles and he smiles at me before jumping off the stage and making his way to me. Sadie and Scarlett cheer.

No. No. No. This can't be happening. I can't resist Miles when he's romantic and sweet. I need to get out of here before I throw myself at him.

My body warms and my nipples tingle as he sings to me about finding a love who is beautiful and sweet from mere feet away. My body obviously doesn't care how hot and cold Miles is. It's ready for me to throw myself at him. Preferably without clothes.

Escape. I need to escape.

Chapter 13

Women want romance, they said. Who are they?

Miles

One minute I'm serenading Hazel and the next she's running away from me. Why is she running? This is supposed to be romantic. She's crazy if she thinks I'll let her go.

I throw the microphone to Sadie. "Catch!"

She fumbles the mic and it clatters to the floor. "Oops! My bad."

She reaches down to pick it up and tumbles to the ground. She stares up at me from where she's sprawled on the floor. "What happened? Why am I on the floor?"

Damn it. I don't have time for this. Hazel is a fast runner *and* she has a headstart. A headstart that's growing by the second.

Scarlett stumbles to her feet. "Go! I've got her."

I hesitate. She doesn't appear to have herself, let alone her little sister. Weston will shoot me in the ass if I let anything happen to his precious woman. And I wouldn't blame him.

I steady Scarlett on her feet. But when I reach down to help Sadie, Alaia elbows me out of the way.

"I've got her. It's not the first time I've picked her up off the floor and it won't be the last."

Despite her words, I don't allow her to drag Sadie from the floor alone. I'm hoping Sadie will be my family at some point in the not too distant future. I can't leave her lying on the floor for someone else to handle.

I grab one side of Sadie while Alaia grabs the other. Together, we manage to set her in a chair.

"What's going on? Why is everyone manhandling me? I'm spoken for. Hands off."

I raise my hands in the air and back away. I didn't realize Sadie was dating anyone, which – considering this small island and its love of gossiping, I should know about – but I know better than to fight with a drunk person. Five brothers taught me my lesson. Multiple times.

"You good?" I ask Scarlett.

"I'm excellent!" Sadie shouts in response. "Hey! Where's Hazel? Did she apparate? I knew it! I knew it was possible. And everyone laughed at me when I read those Harry Potter books."

Scarlett giggles as she waves me away. "Go now before you end up debating the best material to use for a wand."

"You use wood for the wand. Usually holly, yew, or oak. But the unique property is the magical core. It can be from a unicorn, phoenix, or dragon."

"None of which exist!"

I back away. Scarlett has this handled. She sways forward to get in Sadie's face. Crap. Maybe she doesn't have this handled after all.

Alaia pats my arm. "Go after your girl. I already messaged Weston to come and pick them up."

"Thanks."

"No thanks, needed. It's my job. As in it's literally my job."

I flash her another smile of thanks before whirling around to push my way through the crowd. I hesitate. Did Hazel aim for the front door or back? Back. Front is too obvious.

I shoulder my way through the people until I reach the back hallway. I scan the area. The fire alarm didn't go off, so she couldn't have gone through the back door. There are two possibilities – the office or the ladies' room.

I try the door to the office. It opens and I peek inside. Empty.

There's one possibility left. The ladies' room.

I am not barging into the ladies' room. I am not invading anyone's privacy, and I am definitely not pissing off Hazel any more than she already is. Why she's pissed off is a mystery to me, but I'll figure it out.

Soon enough, my Blaze is going to realize I'm not giving up. She should just go ahead and give in now. But my girl doesn't give in. She's a fighter.

I lean against the wall and settle in to wait. A few minutes later, the door opens. Hazel peeks her head out and glowers when she notices me.

I open my arms wide. "Where are you going to go? This isn't the *Bootlegger.* There's no secret exit for you to use in your escape."

She crosses her arms over her chest. "Who says I'm escaping?"

"Me and every single person in the bar."

Her cheeks burn with embarrassment, but she tilts her chin up. There's my girl. She won't let anything in the world get her down. Including me. Too bad she doesn't realize I'm not here to bring her down. I'm here to lift her up.

"What do you want?"

"You." And to find out why she was escaping but 'you' is a correct answer as well.

She huffs. "Are you drunk?"

"No."

"Are you sure? The only time you want me is when you're drunk."

"Wrong. I want you all the time."

She rolls her eyes. "Which is exactly what you say every time you're drunk. And then the next morning, you can't forget my name fast enough."

I growl. "Unfair. You're the one who snuck out of my house on New Year's Day."

She points her finger at me. "You can't complain about me sneaking out."

I raise an eyebrow. "I can't?"

"Nope. Not when I snuck out to avoid the awkward morning after. In fact, you should thank me."

I crowd closer to her. She retreats a few steps until her back hits the wall. "I should thank you for abandoning me?"

Hazel isn't intimidated by me one bit. She narrows her eyes at me. "I didn't abandon you. Ask me how I know."

I don't need to ask. I know exactly what she's referring to. "You can't bring up me breaking up with you when we were twenty every time we argue."

"Yes, I can."

"How are we supposed to build a relationship if you keep bringing up the past? The painful past?"

Her eyes widen, and she rears her head back. "Ouch," she mutters when she hits the wall.

"Are you okay?" I reach to check her for injuries but she bats my hands away.

"I'm fine. Shocked as a mermaid encountering a smuggler in the deep sea, but I'm fine."

"Why are you shocked?"

She snorts. "Are you serious?"

"As a smuggler hiding his loot of moonshine."

"You literally said you want to build a relationship with me."

"It's true. I do."

"Oh, wait." She snaps her fingers. "I'm such an idiot. You don't want a romantic relationship with me. You want a friends with benefits relationship."

I growl and step closer. "I don't want a friends with benefits relationship."

"You don't? If we were friends with benefits – a stupid idea I would never agree to – you could screw around with all the mermaids during Mermaid Karaoke season."

I slap my palms against the wall, boxing her in. "I do not want a mermaid or any other woman. I want you."

"You really are drunk, aren't you?"

"I'm not drunk," I grit out. "I'm finally going after what I want."

"Too bad. You had me and you threw me away."

I lean close and invade her space, being careful not to touch her. "I did not throw you away."

"Oh yeah? How would you name it? You dumped me? You ended our relationship? You ran away from the island to get away from me?"

"I did not run away from you. I would never. But you ran away from me. Why do you keep running away from me?"

Her green eyes flash. "If you think I'm scared of you, you're wrong."

"Of course you aren't scared of me. Hazel Harris isn't afraid of anything. And yet she keeps running away. I'm confused."

A muscle in her jaw ticks. Good. She's getting mad. She can't lie for shit when she's mad.

"I wasn't running away."

I lift an eyebrow. "You jumped to your feet and ran through the crowd."

She shrugs. "Maybe I urgently needed the ladies' room."

"Liar. You can spend all night staking out a house without the need for a ladies' room."

"Because I was too afraid to leave you alone. You were ready to burn some random girl's house down because you thought she hurt your brother."

"I'm not an arsonist."

"Really? And you didn't set fire to your step-dad's house?"

"It was an accident."

"An accident? Sure."

I realize we've gotten so far off track, we're no longer in the stadium. "Why did you run, Blaze?"

Her eyes narrow. "Do not call me Blaze. I am not your Blaze."

"Wrong. You'll always be my Blaze."

She pushes me away and begins to pace the hallway. "This is exactly what I'm talking about. Whenever you drink, you get all sweet and sentimental. All, Blaze, I want you. I can't stand another minute without you. But the second you're sober, you forget I exist. I'm done. I want off the rollercoaster. Not just off. I want a refund. Plus, a payment for damage compensation."

She stops pacing and stands in the middle of the hallway with her legs planted wide and heaving for breath.

"Are you finished?"

"With you? Yep. Done. Dusted. Finito. The end."

I stalk toward her. She backs up until I've got her caged in against the wall.

"We will never be done."

"We already are."

I growl. "No, we aren't."

She opens her mouth to protest but I don't give her the chance. I slam my lips to hers. The second I feel those soft lips against mine, I lose my mind. I thread my fingers through her hair – it's as silky as I remember – and thrust my tongue into her mouth.

She moans and I feel it in my cock. It hardens and lengthens at the feel of Hazel's curves pressing against me. I shove my hardness against her belly and she clings to my shoulders. Her fingernails digging into my skin spurs me on.

I tilt her head to my liking and dive into her mouth. This is what I've been missing. This is what I need. This is—

"Ahem!"

I wrench my mouth from Hazel's to glare at Alaia. She holds up her hands.

"Sorry to interrupt, but I need to get into the office."

I scan the area and realize we're blocking her access. I step backwards, releasing Hazel as I do. She doesn't hesitate. As soon as she's free, she runs off.

Fuck. I'm back to where I started.

Chapter 14

Whose idea was it to build a two-lane bridge anyway?

HAZEL

"I need to do this. This is my best option," I tell myself as I drive over the bridge to leave Smuggler's Hideaway.

An emptiness I can feel in my bones fills me as I arrive on the Mainland and drive further away from my home. If I do this – if I accept this job – Smuggler's Hideaway won't be my home anymore.

Bullshit. It's an hour drive to the VA hospital. I can easily commute one hour each way every day. I'll listen to podcasts or audiobooks. Audiobooks! What a great idea. I never have enough time to read.

This drive won't be so bad after all. For the next fifty minutes, I try to convince myself I can do this. I can become a commuter. It won't be forever.

I frown. Except it will be. It's not as if the population of Smuggler's Hideaway can grow much to provide me with a larger base of potential clients.

Harpoon a mermaid. This would be forever.

I blow out a breath as I turn into the parking lot of the VA hospital. There's no reason to stress myself out about this now. I might not get the job.

As I make my way across the parking lot, I notice everyone is dressed either in military uniform or scrubs. I glance down at my silk blouse, black skirt, and heels. Should I not have worn my interview outfit?

I reach the entrance. Too late now.

The automatic doors open and I step inside the air-conditioned building. Goosebumps form on my arms, but I ignore the cold and march to the reception desk.

I smile at the receptionist. "Good morning. I'm Hazel Harris. I have an appointment with Major Phillips."

"Have a seat. I'll let Major Phillips know you're here."

"Thank you," I murmur before turning around to find a place to sit. I frown. The waiting room is packed. I scan the area until I find an available seat.

I settle myself on the orange plastic chair. I hope I don't have to wait long. This chair is more uncomfortable than sitting in wet sand during a thunderstorm.

"Dude, she's never going to agree to a date with you," the soldier next to me says to his buddy across from him.

"Why not? I've got game."

"You do not have game. You're so far away from having game, you don't know where to find it."

I cough to hide my giggle.

The soldier next to me turns to me. "Hey! You're a woman."

"Last time I checked."

"Help us settle a debate."

"I am not discussing bra sizes or whether big butts are better than flat."

He barks out a laugh before offering me his hand. "Sergeant Barnes."

I shake his hand. "Hazel."

He drops my hand and motions to the soldier across from him. "He's Sergeant Vaquez."

"I thought your name was Sergeant No Game."

I'm full of shit. Barnes and Vaquez are handsome men. Their uniforms strain against their shoulders while their biceps are barely restrained by their short sleeves. Add in their laughing and joking demeanor and I'm certain they don't have any trouble picking up women wherever they happen to find themselves.

Barnes chuckles. "Told you. You have no game."

Vaquez scowls. "Not all of us are bulldozers who think shouting at a woman, 'I'm sexy and I know it,' is okay."

Barnes shrugs. "If it works, it works."

"But does it work?" I ask. "It's pretty cocky."

Barnes winks. "It's okay to be cocky when you can back it up."

"That's not what Tina said," Vaquez says.

I lean forward. "Oh. What did Tina say?"

Vaquez glances around before scooting closer to me. "Apparently, he has a tiny dick."

Barnes kicks his knee. "You've seen my dick. You know it's not tiny. Tina was a bitch." He grimaces. "Sorry, ma'am."

I wave away his apology. "As long as you don't think all women are bitches, we're good."

He leans back in his chair and spreads his legs out before resting his hand on his belt buckle. "Nope. Most women are sweet as pie as long as you know what you're doing."

"And you know what you're doing?"

"I've had a bit of practice." He wiggles his eyebrows.

"Horndog," I mutter.

"What about you? Do you live around here?"

"I'm actually here for a—"

"Ms. Harris," the receptionist calls.

I stand. "That's me."

Barnes and Vaquez stand as well. "It was nice meeting you, ma'am. If you stick around, let us know."

"I haven't gotten my shots yet," I say as I walk away.

Their laughter trails me as I reach the receptionist. She points down the hallway. "Third door on the left."

I knock on the door. "Major Phillips?"

He smiles and rounds his desk to reach me. "Hazel Harris. It's been a while."

I met Major Phillips when I did my internship at the Army Medical Retention Processing Unit back in college. He was a captain then.

I shake his hand. "When did you get stationed here?"

"When I got promoted."

He ushers me to a chair before sitting across from me. "I was surprised to come across your resume. Didn't you say you'd never leave Smuggler's Hideaway?"

"I plan to stay on the island. I can commute."

"That's your choice." He snatches a stack of papers off his desk. "Now, tell me what you've been doing since you graduated."

I clear my throat. "I started my own practice on Smuggler's Hideaway."

"Impressive. Having your own practice. Why would you want to give it up to come work for us?"

This is where things get tricky. How to sell myself to this man without making myself appear to be a loser who can't build a PT practice.

"Major! Major!" An elderly man says as he rushes into the room.

"What is it, Frank?"

Frank notices me and stumbles to a halt. "Are you busy?"

"I'm always busy, Frank. But it never stops you."

"Do you work here?" Frank asks me.

"Not if I can't finish this interview."

"Oh, sorry. I didn't realize. I better go. I wouldn't want this pretty young thing to tank her interview." His eyes sparkle. "We can always use more pretty things to look at around here."

"I'm happy to oblige."

"Oh, she's good. You should hire her, Major."

The major sighs. "I need to interview her first."

"Right you are." Frank salutes before pivoting toward the door.

"Frank," the major calls before he reaches it, "did you have a reason for interrupting me?"

"Shoot. I nearly forgot. The vending machine's out of pretzels again. You know how much I enjoy those little pretzels."

"I'll notify Command."

Once Frank wanders off, Major Phillips stands and shuts the door behind him. "Let's see how long we last before the next interruption." He sits across from me again. "You were telling me about your practice back home."

"Yes, Major, I—"

"Ed. You're not in the military. Feel free to call me Ed."

I smile. "Okay, Ed."

For the next thirty minutes, I explain my situation while Ed asks me questions. When he stands to end the interview, I feel pretty good about how it went.

"If I could hire you right now, I would. Unfortunately, bureaucracy."

Yes! Told you I nailed the interview. I'd do a fist pump but it's not professional. I clear my throat.

"I understand." I shake his hand before saying goodbye.

I sing along to the radio as I drive toward Smuggler's Hideaway. This could work. I could drive to the VA hospital every day.

The job is awesome. I love working with military men and women. They're always super motivated. And Ed is great. He has tons of experience as a physical therapist. I could learn a lot from him.

I'm fifteen minutes out from the island when the cars in front of me come to a complete standstill. What in the name of mermaids frolicking in the sea is happening? I strain my neck to peer past the cars in front of me, but all I see is more cars. Was there an accident?

I tap my fingers on the steering wheel as I wait for some movement. I need to be at the restaurant soon. I can't be late today. I'm opening.

After a few minutes, the car ahead of me starts to move. At a snail's pace. I'm barely going five miles per hour. And then – boom! – we grind to a halt again.

As long as we're stopped, I figure it's safe to check my app for a reason why there's so much traffic. I scroll through until I find a notification about this highway.

Heavy congestion ahead. Expect a twenty-minute delay at Smuggler's Hideaway Bridge.Cause: Tourists.

Tourists? It's not even tourist season yet, and the traffic is horrible. How bad will it be in the summer? It'll take me two hours to get home from the hospital.

Smoking smugglers. Maybe I can't commute to the hospital. Maybe I'll have to move after all.

But do I want to move when Miles recently proclaimed his intention to build a relationship with me? I purse my lips. I can't believe what he said. He's always claiming his love and desire for me when he's drunk. And then, when he's sober, he forgets all about his claims.

I guess it's time to seriously consider leaving the island.

Chapter 15

Why couldn't I have had sisters instead of brothers?

MILES

I grab my rabbit's foot from the passenger seat before folding out of my car. I stare at Eli's house as I walk up the driveway. It's easy to forget he's a billionaire when we're working at the distillery. But, at his mansion, his wealth is undeniable.

I don't need wealth. Hell, I was happy with my surf shack being an actual shack until a hurricane came along and blew it over. Eli insisted on building a more 'substantial' structure. I wasn't going to stop him.

I greet my brothers with a wave when I enter. It appears I'm the last person to arrive, which isn't unusual since I hate being on time. Kai used to be worse than me until he fell in love with Harper. Now, he's Mr. Punctual. Annoying.

Zane smiles at Kai. "You owe me."

Kai slaps a bill in his hand. "I'm disappointed in you, Miles."

"In me?" I tap my chest. "What did I do?"

"It's what you didn't do. I assumed you'd spend another night serenading Hazel. You're never going to win her back if you're here playing poker with us."

"Poker night is mandatory for all Raider brothers."

I'm not making this rule up. Our monthly poker nights are mandatory. The only exceptions are – your partner is having a baby, or you're in the hospital. Being sick is not sufficient. Especially since Eli's house has enough bathrooms to allow us each to have our own. Trust me. It's been necessary in the past.

Jaxon clears his throat. "I should make a rule. During the wooing phase of seduction, a Raider brother can skip poker."

Since Jaxon has a hard time feeling he's part of the group, Rhett and Eli came up with the idea of allowing him to make one arbitrary rule per poker night.

Rhett grunts. "No fair. Miles is the only Raider brother still in the wooing phase."

"Plus, you're no longer allowed to make poker rules," Eli adds.

Jaxon frowns. "I'm not?"

"Not since the last time you made a rule and Zane ended up beyond wasted. He peed in the azaleas. Paisley's still mad at me."

Zane's nose wrinkles. "I don't remember peeing in the azaleas."

I chuckle. "You were pretty drunk."

He scowls. "I had to drink a shot of moonshine every time I mentioned my daughter. Which was bullshit."

"You say bullshit, I say hilarious."

Zane found out literally minutes before the poker game that Adele was his biological daughter. He was beaming with happiness. Naturally, we couldn't allow his happiness to go unpunished.

"Speaking of moonshine." Eli indicates the shots lined up at the bar.

I hold up my hands. "No moonshine for me. I'm on a strict beer diet tonight."

Jaxon pushes his glasses up his nose. "Does this have anything to do with Hazel?"

Rhett slaps him on the back. "Of course, this has something to do with Hazel."

"How?" Jaxon asks me.

I don't bother hesitating. My brothers will get the information out of me eventually anyway. And I have no desire to spend tomorrow hungover or picking glitter out of my underwear. Trust me. No man wants the man next to him at the urinals to start sprouting glitter.

"Hazel thinks I only want her when I'm drinking."

Eli narrows his eyes on me. "Do you?"

"Do I what?"

"Only want her when you're drinking? You've been home from Hawaii for six years and haven't made any moves to win her back in all this time."

Because I've been a fucking idiot who thought that when I finally figured out my life, Hazel would be there waiting for me.

Zane barks out a laugh. "Except he follows her around like a puppy dog whenever she's in the same room as him."

"And chases her when she runs away," Kai adds.

"And don't forget the times he managed to con her back into his bed," Rhett says.

I scowl. "I've never conned Hazel in my life."

He lifts an eyebrow. "You have sex with her every few months and then disappear from her life. Pretty sure that's the definition of conning."

"I don't disappear from her life."

"Really? You don't avoid her for a few weeks before starting this whole cycle back up again?"

Jaxon fiddles with his glasses. "Convincing Hazel to give you another chance is not going to be easy. We should brainstorm some ideas."

"I don't need my brothers to help me come up with ideas."

Rhett crosses his arms over his chest. "You don't? You've already figured out a way to win Hazel back?"

No. But I know better than to follow any advice they give me. Their advice will be designed to humiliate me. Not help me. It's the same thing I'd do if I was in their position.

"I have an idea," Jaxon says.

"I told you. I don't need your ideas."

He ignores me and continues. "It sounds as if you're using Hazel."

I growl. "I'm not using her."

He holds up a hand. "I didn't say you were. I said it sounds as if you are."

"What's your point?"

"You should tell her no sex."

"Hypocrite," Rhett coughs.

"I admit I had sex with Blossom when our marriage was fake. But we're not discussing me. We're discussing Miles."

"Why are we discussing my love life anyway?" I ask the room.

Kai chuckles. "I think you mean your life of celibacy."

Zane laughs before high-fiving him.

I glare at them. "Are we going to play poker or stand around and gossip like old women all night?"

"Old men enjoy gossiping as well," Rhett says.

"Whatever. Are we playing poker or not?"

Eli slaps my back. "I'm happy to take your money any day."

"I'm not the brother who always loses at poker." I point to Zane.

"I lost on purpose but not anymore." He rubs his hands together. "Now Daddy needs a new rocking chair."

Eli leads us down the hallway to the game room. If the size of the house didn't give away how much money my big brother has, this room would. It's decorated like a magazine spread with leather couches for watching football games, a gleaming wooden bar stocked with every liquor you can imagine, and a television larger than anything I've ever seen in a private house before.

We make our way to the poker table in the middle of the room next to the pool table and take our seats. Everyone sets their lucky charm down on the table in front of them. A lucky charm is another one of the 'requirements' for poker night.

"When are the rest of you going to get normal lucky charms?"

"What do you mean?" Kai asks. "Mr. Crisp is a perfectly normal lucky charm."

"Except he's a pickle in a jar you're convinced can talk to you."

He rolls his eyes. "He doesn't talk to me. He gives me vibes I interpret."

Eli walks to the bar to get everyone's drinks. Rhett sets his good luck charm – one bowling shoe, since he lost the other one – down before picking up the deck of cards and inspecting it.

"Whatcha doing?" Kai asks in a voice he thinks sounds innocent. It doesn't. Not since every brother in this room knows he's the farthest thing from innocent.

Rhett glares at him. "Making sure this deck isn't oozing with maple syrup or honey or whatever sticky material you prefer."

"It's a new deck."

"It's always a new deck." Considering the amount of pranks we play on each other, using a new deck every poker night is a necessity.

"You're good," Eli says as he returns with several beers. "I got this deck out of my safe before everyone arrived."

"Wonderful." Jaxon rubs his hands together. "The Green King and I are ready to win."

The Green King is his lucky charm. It's a Chia Pet, he claims resembles Elvis. It doesn't. It's a lump.

"Too bad Nugget and I are going to kick your ass." Zane rubs a hand over the back of his taxidermized squirrel in a cowboy hat. Told you my brothers have weird ass good luck charms.

Rhett finishes dealing and it quiets down while everyone studies their cards. Time to play some poker.

"I fold." The cards have not been my friends tonight. I've lost the last three rounds.

Kai chuckles. "Pretty sure you already folded when you threw your cards at Eli's face the previous go-around."

"He shouldn't have snapped those freaky fake teeth at me." I shiver. Eli's good luck charm of fake teeth freaks me out. He used to chase us around the house with them when we were kids. I had nightmares about those teeth.

"I win this round." Jaxon lays his cards on the table.

"How the hell do you have a straight flush?" Rhett asks.

Jaxon shrugs as he draws all the poker chips to him and begins sorting them. I frown at the amount of chips he has compared to me. Tonight is not my night.

Rhett deals another round of cards and I bite my tongue to stop my groan at my cards. Time for desperate measures.

I inch my phone out of my pocket and wake it. After Eli and Rhett have their turns, I increase the sound and hit the app.

Chirp! Chirp! Chirp! Chirp!

Eli jumps to his feet. "Smoke alarm. Everyone out."

Everyone grabs their beers and lucky charms before filing out of the room to the front exit. Once we're on the porch with Paisley, who's holding baby Stephanie, Eli phones his security company to let them know about the alarm.

I wait until he hangs up the phone and jump off the porch. "You've been pranked!" I yell before sprinting to my car. Zane and Kai give chase but with my headstart I easily beat them to my car.

I fold into the driver's seat and back out of the drive while rolling down the window.

"I'm winning the prank war!" I yell before driving away.

Chapter 16

Miles is more tempting than the promise of a chocolate cake with no calories.

Hazel

I'm washing my hands after my patient left my practice when I hear the bell above the door ring. Miles is here.

Heat flushes through my body as butterflies erupt in my stomach. Miles is here for a PT session. I can put my hands on his skin, smell his scent, and enjoy how handsome he is. I place a hand over my stomach and tell it to calm down.

But it's Miles.

It doesn't matter. Miles doesn't want me.

He says he does. He serenaded you. Chased you. More than once. Claimed he wants a relationship.

I force those thoughts away. All typical Miles actions after a night of drinking. It's not real.

If I'm starting a relationship with someone, it has to be real. The man has to be reliable. Not a man who switches from hot to cold so fast it would give a mermaid whiplash.

Besides, I'm probably leaving the island anyway. Long distance relationships don't work. It's one of the million reasons Miles gave for dumping me when he left for the surfing pro tour stop in Hawaii.

I blow out a breath, square my shoulders, and walk to the reception area. Miles smiles at me and those blue eyes of his sparkle.

"Hi, Blaze."

His deep voice has goosebumps exploding over my skin. Be a professional, Hazel. This is your workplace. Not a bar. Except… my brow wrinkles.

"Are you carrying a bottle of moonshine?" I check the time. "At ten in the morning."

His cheeks darken. "I made it for you."

I blink. "You made me moonshine?"

He clears his throat. "It's a mixture I developed for you. I'm calling it Ginger Siren."

"What's in it?"

"It's a bold, fiery blend with notes of ginger heat, island zest, and smooth molasses sweetness."

Huh. It actually sounds good. "Shall we taste it?"

"I thought you'd never ask." He grins before pulling two shot glasses out of his backpack.

I giggle. "You brought shot glasses to therapy?"

"I wanted you to have the chance to try the moonshine I created for you."

Those butterflies are back in my stomach, flapping their wings, but I ignore them. He made me moonshine. It's not a big deal.

Except he hates working at the distillery.

He hands me a shot glass before raising his in the air. He meets my gaze before toasting, "Here's to the mermaids and the smugglers who loved them."

This isn't the Smuggler's Hideaway toast. The Smuggler's Hideaway toast is *Here's to the smugglers, bootleggers, rumrunners, and the mermaids who loved them.* But he switched things around. Is he trying to tell me something?

"Go ahead." He nudges my hand. "Try it."

I drink the shot. The liquid burns as it travels down my esophagus. But not the good moonshine burn. It's pure fire. My chest is on fire. My nostrils are on fire. I cough and slap my chest in an effort to put the flames out.

"What the hell did you put in this?" I ask when I can finally speak again.

"Fresh ginger, molasses, citrus zest, cinnamon, cloves, chili flakes, and an experimental yeast strain from *Five Fathoms.*"

"I don't know what's more disturbing. The list of ingredients or you borrowing an experimental yeast strain."

"I wanted to speed up fermentation. Today's our last PT session. This is a thank you gift for you agreeing to work with me despite not wanting to."

"The next time you want to give me a gift, don't. Just don't."

"I want to shower you with gifts."

My brow wrinkles. "You were never one to give gifts without reason before."

He scowls. "Because I didn't have the money before."

I match his scowl. "And since you're now the sales manager for a successful distillery, you're going to shove your money in my face."

"I'm not shoving my money in your face."

"Not with moonshine that tastes like someone mugged a gingerbread man and drowned him in floor cleaner, you aren't."

"Are you saying you wouldn't mug a gingerbread man with me?"

I gasp. "I would never mug a gingerbread man."

Miles snorts. "And you wouldn't steal from Santa Claus either."

I wag my finger at him. "It was your fault."

He clutches his chest. "How was it my fault?"

"You tackled the elf."

He growls. "The elf slapped your ass."

"You gave him a bloody nose."

"He deserved it."

"They were going to arrest you. I was forced to steal from Santa Claus to give you a chance to escape."

"It's a good thing you're a fast runner."

"I circled around and gave Santa all his money back."

He rolls his eyes. "Of course, you did, Blaze."

Those butterflies in my stomach love him using his nickname for me. I know better. Miles talks the talk, but he doesn't walk the walk.

"Miles, I'm not your Blaze anymore."

"But you can be again. I want you to be again." He steps closer and tucks a strand of hair behind my ear. "What do you want?"

I want to believe him. More than anything I've ever wanted before. But I don't. I don't trust Miles. He's not a stayer. He's a leaver. The first time he left me nearly killed me. I don't think I can survive a second time.

"I don't want to get my heart broken again." My eyes widen when I realize what I said. "Not that you can break my heart. I won't let you. I'm not starting a relationship knowing it's a dead end."

"We are not a dead end," he grumbles.

"Agree to disagree." I clear my throat. "Now, are we doing some PT or what?"

He stares at me for a long moment and I hold my breath. I don't know how long I can resist Miles. I've never been good at resisting him before. Which is how I ended up in this whole mess in the first place. But resist him I must.

"Sure. What are we doing today?"

I allow the tension in my body to release before answering, "Strengthening exercises and targeted training. I want to make sure your rotator cuff is as strong as it can be since surfing season is coming up."

"It's always surfing season."

I snort. "If you can afford to travel all over the world chasing waves."

"I don't have time to travel the world. Business is booming at *Buccaneer's Whiskey & Distillery*."

I lead him to the largest room in my practice with all of the rehab equipment. "You don't seem happy about business booming."

I motion for him to lie on the exercise bench. Once he's lying on his side with his affected arm on top, I hand him a weight.

"I thought I was going to spend my career surfing. But thanks to this." He nods to his shoulder. "I work in an office. I hate sitting behind my desk."

"Start lifting," I order him before continuing our conversation. "But you're the sales manager. Don't sales managers charm the customers on golfing excursions?"

He chuckles. "Not in the twenty-first century. Now all contact can be handled by email and phone calls."

"Really? You don't need to travel to the mainland occasionally to charm distributors or handle the big accounts?"

He frowns. "Eli has been charming distributors and handling the big accounts."

I tap his shoulder to indicate he can take a break. "Maybe you should discuss this with your big brother."

He offers me the weight and I hand him a resistance band. "Same exercise but with a resistance band this time."

He groans. "I'm glad today is my last day."

I frown. "If you aren't doing these exercises at home, I'm not signing you off."

"You're welcome to come to my home and check on me. I'll leave the light on for you." He waggles his eyebrows.

"Home visits cost extra."

His eyes flare. "I promise to make it worth your while."

My nipples harden at the promise in his voice. I am well acquainted with how well Miles can make it worth my while.

"Miles," I scold but I'm afraid I sound out of breath and excited.

"Sorry, Blaze. I shouldn't tempt you."

I narrow my eyes. "Tempt me? Why do you think you can tempt me?"

He smirks. "Experience."

"Time's up!"

"But I only did two exercises."

"Patients don't usually complain about only doing two exercises."

"Those patients don't want to soak up every possible second with you."

Damn it. He went from sexy to sweet. I have a hard time resisting either Miles, but sweet Miles is especially difficult to resist.

I slap my hand on the bench. "Get going or I'll charge you for another session."

"As much as I'd love another session, I need to get back to work. I need to finish a management report today."

I follow him to the door and watch him leave. Once he's out of sight, I collapse against the door. Phew. Close call.

I should probably avoid Miles until I can build up some resistance to him. I haven't managed to build up any resistance in the past six years, but I wasn't trying too hard. Not when I knew Miles didn't want me. Now, my heart's survival depends on it.

Chapter 17

Thank you, giant anchor in the sky.

Miles

"You made it!" Harper squeals, and I glance over my shoulder. Phew. Hazel came. I wasn't certain she would. She's jumpier than a smuggler who just spotted a Prohi.

Hazel scans the interior of *The Drunken Anchor Lanes* and frowns when her gaze lands on me. "I've been scammed," she mutters before whirling around toward the exit.

I rush to intercept her. "Blaze, wait!'

She fists her hands on her hips. "Give me one reason why I shouldn't leave now."

"Because it's *Sirens & Strikes Night* and I know how much you enjoy it."

"So you asked your sister-in-law to invite me?"

I stuff my hands in my pockets and shrug. "I didn't think you'd say yes if I invited you."

"Miles, your whole family is here," she hisses instead of answering my question, which is kind of an answer.

"You love my family."

When we were dating way back in high school, Hazel spent nearly as much time at my house as she did at hers. She laughed and joked with my brothers and helped Mom prepare meals. She was a part of our family.

Until I went and screwed it all up. But she will be a part of our family again. I will do everything in my power to convince her to give me a second chance.

She blows out a breath. "And you're deliberately misunderstanding my point."

"Not deliberately. I don't understand your point."

"Your family will think we're back together."

"Would it be so bad if we were back together?" I hold my breath as I wait for her answer.

"Miles."

I step closer. "Everyone in my family knows I want a second chance with you. They also know you haven't given me one yet."

"They're also staring at us."

"You can't be surprised. My brothers are as nosy as you are."

Her jaw drops open. "Me? Nosy?"

I snort. "Did you or did you not end up with detention in freshman year for eavesdropping on the principal?"

"Is it eavesdropping when she's screaming loud enough for everyone on the island to hear?"

"It is when you stick your ear to a glass against her door.'

"Whatever."

"Come on." I motion to the lanes. "It'll be fun. I already spotted the contraband item in our lane. I bet you can't knock it loose."

Sirens & Strikes Night isn't your usual bowling night. Each lane has a hidden 'contraband item' — toy rum barrels, fake gold coins, a mini anchor. If your ball knocks it loose, you win a prize.

Hazel's eyes narrow on mine. I've got her now and she knows it. She can't resist a challenge.

"When I knock the contraband item loose, you have to parade around *Drunken Anchor Lanes* clucking like a chicken."

I'd parade around the lanes naked with my face painted purple, if it would get her to stay. I hold out my hand. "You're on."

As soon as she shakes my hand, I usher her forward. "We have lanes six and seven."

"Brave. Lane seven is cursed."

"It's not cursed just because you always lose when you bowl on lane seven."

She glares at me. "I do not always lose on lane seven."

I lift an eyebrow. "You don't?"

"Stop challenging me."

I chuckle. "But it's fun."

"How about another bet?"

My brothers inch closer – they're addicted to betting – but I motion for them to stay where they are. This is between Blaze and me.

"Name your bet."

"If I win, you have to sing *I Believe In A Thing Called Love* over the intercom."

I groan. "I can't sing that song."

She giggles. "I know. I remember you trying to sing it at Mermaid Karaoke. You were booed off the stage."

Not one of my proudest moments but Kai dared me. I don't turn down a dare any more than Hazel refuses a challenge.

"You want everyone to boo me."

She shrugs. "If you're a loser…"

I narrow my eyes at her. "If you lose, you have to attend one of my surfing classes."

Hazel is not a fan of surfing. She enjoys watching it, but she hates getting too far out in the ocean where all the 'vicious animals' are. She's never recovered from the *Jaws* marathon we watched when she was fourteen.

She shivers. "Fine, but if the sharks eat me, I am going to return as a poltergeist and haunt the mermaid out of you."

"If you can knock on windows or throw objects, you're totally haunting your brothers."

She sniffs. "I can haunt you *and* my brothers at the same time. I'm a woman. I can multi-task."

"No shark is going to eat you anyway."

She smirks. "Because you're not going to win."

"Game on, Blaze. Game on." I place my hand on her lower back to lead her to the lane. She gasps at my touch and I duck my chin to hide my smile. She still wants me, but she's being cautious. And stubborn. I'm not worried. I can out stubborn Hazel any day of the week.

We join my family at lane seven, and the lights begin to flash.

"The pins aren't the only things going down tonight," the DJ declares.

Eli hands out shot glasses filled with moonshine.

"To the bootleggers!" The DJ hollers before the lights go out. Our glow-in-the-dark shots provide the only illumination.

"Masters of the sneaky snips and secret stashes. Thanks for keeping the party alive," we toast before drinking our shots and the lights blink on again.

Hazel slams her shot glass down on the table. "That was way better than whatever moonshine Miles tried to poison me with the other day."

I frown. "I wasn't trying to poison you."

She blinks. "Oh, it was a lucky side effect?"

"Lucky?" I snort. "I think not. Do you not remember when you got food poisoning junior year and moved into the bathroom for two days?"

"Dad was not amused. One bathroom for six people is not enough."

We sit down to change into our bowling shoes. Everyone who grew up on the island has their own pair since bowling is the most popular gym course during senior year of high school.

Hazel wanders off to find a bowling ball. I can't help but watch her. She smiles at everyone, stops to talk to people she knows, and generally spreads joy wherever she goes. I need her to aim some of that joy my way.

Zane sits next to me and bumps my shoulder. "You've got it bad."

I elbow him. "You promised to behave tonight."

He jumps to his feet. "Too bad you never defined behave."

Jaxon frowns. "Classic mistake."

I shoo him away. "Aren't you on lane six?"

"Come on." Blossom grasps his arm. "We'll be out of the danger zone but still within the watching zone."

Hazel skips back to our lane with her bowling ball. "I hope you're ready to parade around clucking like a chicken."

I tug on one of her curls. "You need to knock the contraband item loose first."

"How hard can it be? There's a toy rum barrel in the middle of the lane. I'll knock it loose on my first try."

I motion her forward. "By all means."

She stands at the end of the lane and tilts her head from side to side as she studies the best way to hit the toy rum barrel. After a minute, she nods and raises her ball into the air. She takes two steps and an alarm sounds as a giant anchor slowly lowers from the ceiling.

Everyone in the bowling alley freezes. If you move while the anchor is lowered, you get a gutter penalty. And everyone heckles you.

"You moved!" Sloane points to Hazel.

"Anchor breaker!" Zane chants, and soon enough, everyone is chanting with him. "Anchor breaker! Anchor breaker!"

"I didn't move. I got a cramp!" Hazel exclaims before stomping over to put her ball in the ball return.

She collapses on the chair next to me and I hand her a shot. "Bottoms up, anchor breaker."

She narrows her eyes at me before she raises the shot glass and drinks the moonshine. "I was in the middle of my approach. It's impossible to stop on a moment's notice."

I pat her arm. "Sure, it is."

"Don't patronize me."

"It means to treat in a way that appears kind or helpful but betrays a feeling of superiority," Jaxon says from the lane next to ours.

I give him the finger. "I'm not an idiot."

He fiddles with his glasses. "You're not?"

Hazel bursts into laughter. "I forgot how much fun your family is."

"You should give Miles a second chance," Sloane says.

"And then you can be part of the family," Harper finishes.

"How much did you pay them to say that?" Hazel asks.

"Nothing," I claim at the same moment Sloane says, "A weekend of babysitting."

Hazel's eyes widen. "You're going to babysit for a weekend?"

I wasn't planning on it since I never agreed to babysit baby Adele but her surprise has me scowling. "I can babysit. I'm responsible."

"Miles Raider is going to miss a weekend of surfing to babysit?"

"You make it sound as if I spend every single moment in the surf."

She lifts an eyebrow. "Don't you? After all – there's nothing more important."

"Wrong," I grumble. "I can give you a list of things more important than surfing – starting with spending time with you and ending with spending time with you."

Her eyes dilate, but she shakes her head. "You've been drinking again."

I bite my tongue before I growl. I'm about done with her thinking the only reason I want her is because I'm drunk. I've proven otherwise but she's still skittish.

"I had one shot of moonshine. Nothing more. But if you don't believe me, you can message Weston and have him come here and do a sobriety test."

She rolls her eyes. "Please, we spent a month practicing the walk-and-turn and one-leg stand until we could do it while completely smashed. A sobriety test means nothing."

"I meant a breathalyzer."

"You would do a breathalyzer test right here, right now?"

"Yep."

"You haven't been drinking?"

I guide my finger down her cheek. "I told you, Blaze. I want you. I want my second chance with you. I'll do whatever you need me to, to prove I'm worthy of a second chance."

She nibbles on her bottom lip as she studies me. I want to be the one nibbling on her lip while my fingers thread through her silky hair.

But there's more to us than our chemistry. So I inhale a deep breath and keep my hands to myself.

"You surprise me, Miles."

"If you let me, I'll surprise you every single day for the rest of our lives."

"The rest of our lives?"

I shrug. "Or until we're senile."

"Miles!" Kai shouts. "It's your turn."

"There's no rush, Blaze. Take your time and think about what I said."

I wait for her nod before I stand and saunter away. I will continue to push her, but it's enough for today. I don't want to overwhelm her. I want her to have fun. She deserves to have all the fun in her life.

Chapter 18

This surfing lesson did not end the way I intended.

Hazel

"This is ridiculous," I mutter as I make my way through the sand to Miles's surf shack.

I can't believe I have to take a surfing lesson because I lost at bowling. Which wasn't my fault. Lane seven is cursed. If we had any other lane, I would have won no problem.

When I reach the shack, a crowd has already gathered. A crowd of women wearing the tiniest bikinis in existence. I frown down at my swimming outfit – a pair of surf shorts and a t-shirt that doubles as a swimming top. I'm frumpy and old compared to these bronze-skinned, blonde women.

The door to the surf shack opens and Miles steps out. The women immediately flock to him. He scans the area until his gaze meets mine. He smiles before approaching me.

He kisses my forehead. "Are you okay?"

I scowl at him. "Why wouldn't I be okay? Because you're a cheater?"

He chuckles. "I'm not a cheater because you lost."

"The anchor just happened to lower every time I was on approach."

"As much as it pains me to admit this, I did not have any control over the anchor."

I groan. "You've tried to control the anchor in the past, haven't you?"

"The owners of *The Drunken Anchor Lanes* are mean. They keep everything under lock and key. And they put pictures of me and my brothers up everywhere to warn their workers about the Raider brothers as if we're wanted criminals."

"You probably deserved it."

He frowns. "It's not my fault, I accidentally broke the pin-setter. Zane's the one who threw two balls at the same time. I was merely trying to make sure everything reset properly."

"And maybe screw Zane's score at the same time."

He shrugs. "It's my moral imperative as his older brother to screw with him as much as possible."

"Good to know some things never change."

"Miles," a woman approaches while hollering his name, "are we starting the lesson soon?" She presses her breasts against his arm as she voices her question.

Miles steps away without bothering to check out her cleavage. "Pick out a board. We'll start soon."

She bats her eyelashes at him. "Will you help me pick one out?"

"They're all the same." He shackles my wrist. "Come on. I want you next to me."

I tug on my wrist but he holds on tight. "Miles, let me go."

He draws me closer to whisper in my ear. "Please don't abandon me alone with her. It's the second time this week Tiffany has taken this course. She's a maneater."

I giggle. "Are you afraid of a woman?"

He glares at me. "Are you afraid of sharks?"

"Not fair. Sharks are literally maneaters. They have sharp teeth and those beady eyes." I shiver.

"One day I'll get you out in the surf zone and you are going to love it."

I snort. "And one day the doctor will prescribe the correct medicine to cure you of those delusions."

He smiles and those blue eyes twinkle. "My Blaze can do anything she wants to."

His Blaze? A shiver rolls down my spine at the idea of being his again. But it's an illusion. Miles is not to be trusted.

"Too bad, I don't want to surf."

"You'll change your mind." He tweaks my nose. Before I can respond, he whips off his t-shirt and I forget how to use words.

Miles has always had the sexiest upper body of any man I've ever seen. And I've seen a lot, considering I live on a popular tourist island where men think walking around without a shirt is attractive. It's not. Unless your name is Miles.

His shoulders are broad and strong. You wouldn't know he has a weak shoulder due to an injury to his rotator cuff. His chest is muscular but not overly defined like those men who live in the gym. No, Miles's muscles are bred from his love of surfing.

And then there are his abs. Those ridges I love to touch and lick. I love to feel them move beneath my hands when I touch him. The way they harden when he gets excited.

"What's wrong?" Miles asks and I drag my eyes up his body to his face. "Mermaid got your tongue?"

I flick my hair over my shoulder. "Isn't this what I'm supposed to do at one of your famous surfing lessons? Objectify you, surfer boy, and hope you'll choose me as the favored one?"

His eyes darken before he steps closer. "I will always choose you, Blaze. Each and every time. Until I'm old and gray and don't remember which end of the surfing board enters the water first."

Welp. My teasing backfired. Miles is supposed to be bantering with me. Not making my panties damp.

"Miles!" another woman yells. "We're ready."

Miles eyes flash with annoyance before he blinks and it's gone. "We'll get started in one minute, Brittany."

I glance over my shoulder to discover Brittany is another blonde wearing a tiny bikini.

"Do those bikinis hold up in the surf?"

Miles grimaces. "You're cruel."

I blink and widen my eyes to feign innocence. "Whatever do you mean?"

"You're the only woman I want to see lose her bikini."

"Not wearing a bikini."

He squeezes my hip. "Still the sexiest woman here."

He claps his hands to get everyone's attention. Once the women quiet down, he begins with a safety briefing. I should probably pay attention – sharks and currents are no joke – but who in their right mind can pay attention when Miles is strutting around without a shirt on in front of them? I'm not that strong.

"Are there any questions?" he asks once he's finished.

Tiffany throws her hand in the air and jumps up and down. Uh oh. Her bikini top is barely holding on. But Miles doesn't pay her top any attention. He gazes off in the distance.

"Is it true wax for surfboards is called sex wax?"

"Sex Wax is a brand. Any more questions?" When Tiffany jumps up and down again, he ignores her. "Any questions on the safety briefing?"

"Okay. Moving on. We'll practice paddling and the 'pop-up' technique for standing on dry land before moving to the water to catch small, broken waves close to shore."

"Can't we go out further?" Brittany asks.

"Not today. Today's a beginner class. If you want to go out further, you can join an advanced class."

"But all of us have done the beginner class already this week."

Miles motions to me. "Hazel hasn't."

"Can't she wait on the shore or something?"

He growls. "Hazel isn't waiting on the shore. She waits for no one."

"Whatever."

When no one else speaks up, Miles proceeds to run us through a bunch of exercises for paddling and popping up. It's not long before he's telling us to pick up our boards and get into the water.

The other women shriek as they rush into the water to play in the waves. I'm less excited about this part. I carry my board into the water until I'm waist deep. I sit on the board and dangle my legs in the water.

"You should be laying down on your board," Miles says as he joins me.

I wag my finger at him. "Only if I want to catch a wave."

"Which is the entire purpose of a surfing class."

"I agreed to attend a surfing class if I lost at bowling – which I didn't, since you cheated – I didn't agree to actually surf."

"There's nothing to compare to the feeling of standing on your board racing a wave."

"I'm good." I motion to the tiny bikini brigade. "Don't you want to go help the other students?"

"Nope. I want to stay right here with you."

"But they'll write you a bad review."

He snorts. "They'll write me a bad review anyway unless I flirt with them."

My stomach sours. This is what Miles's life is. Flirting with pretty college students. Probably taking one home more often than I care to know about. This is why I can't give him a chance. I can't trust him.

Except he hasn't responded to any of their flirting today. He's kept his attention focused on me.

"Hey!" Miles squeezes my thigh to bring me closer. "Where did you go?"

I scan the horizon. "Pretty sure I haven't gone anywhere since I refuse to go any deeper into the water."

He glides his hand up and down my thigh. I nearly moan at the feel of his hand on me. His hands are big and strong. And yet gentle enough to bring me pleasure.

"Blaze, where did you go in your head?"

I sigh and give in. I might as well tell him. Maybe then he'll understand why us dating is such a bad idea. "Thinking about all the college students you've flirted with in the past."

"I'm not going to deny flirting with women in the past. It would be an insult to your intelligence. But I'm not a player. I'm not Zane. I don't have sex with every woman I flirt with." He clears his throat. "In fact, I haven't had sex with any other woman for over a year."

My mouth drops open. "Over a year?"

His cheeks darken. "No woman has interested me."

"Except me?"

His gaze lifts to meet mine. "Always you, Blaze."

"Miles!" Tiffany screams and Miles grunts. "I better go help her. You okay here on your own?"

"I can literally touch the sand with my toes."

He squeezes my thigh before rushing off to help Tiffany.

As I watch, I notice how he avoids touching her and moves out of the way every time she tries to touch him. He wasn't lying. He's not interested in another woman. Not even when he could easily touch her in the name of 'teaching'.

Silly sirens in the sea. I'm going to give in to him, aren't I? I'm going to give Miles a second chance.

It'll be fine. He won't break my heart. He's going to screw things up soon enough anyway. A few dates won't hurt. It'll be a bit of fun. Nothing more. Certainly nothing serious.

Chapter 19

Best surprise ever.

MILES

Relief smacks into me when I finally shake off the surfing class students and their advances to find Hazel putting the gear into the surf shack.

I'm surprised she didn't run away. Although, she's running away from me less and less. Sometimes, I get the feeling her resistance to me is fading. Other times, her eyes dart around the room as if she's searching for an exit or a rabbit hole to dive down.

"This brings back memories, doesn't it?"

She scowls. "I am not having sex in your surf shack for old times' sake."

Damn. Those are some good memories. But not what I meant.

"I didn't mean the times we snuck out here to fool around. I mean, all the times you waited for me after practice and helped me pick up my gear."

"Oh."

I tweak her nose. "Oh."

We finish putting things away in silence. Not an awkward silence. This is comfortable. Like slipping into an old hoodie to watch a football game. Familiar but with a spark of anticipation.

"This place has certainly improved," Hazel says while I lock up.

"The original shack blew away in the hurricane. Eli insisted on building me a sturdier structure."

"I'm sorry about the original shack."

I shrug. "Thanks."

I begin walking toward the parking lot and she falls into step with me. We walk in synch. As if those years we were separated never happened.

"Do you need a ride?"

"Nah. I'm good. My apartment isn't far."

I notice she's shivering and frown. "Are you cold?" I don't wait for an answer before whipping off my hoodie and placing it over her head.

"I'm not five. I can dress myself."

I help her put her arms through the sleeves. "Maybe. But then I wouldn't get the pleasure of touching you."

She sniffs the sweatshirt and I glance away before she notices my smile. Her resistance to me is definitely fading.

"Speaking of touching…"

"Yes?" I ask when she doesn't continue.

She fiddles with the hem of my sweatshirt. I don't push her. Pushing Hazel never works. She's more likely to become contrary and smack me with a firework than agree with me.

I slow my steps to give her time to gather her thoughts. We're nearly at my car when she finally speaks.

"I was thinking about that second chance you want."

My heart lodges in my throat. Is she serious? Is she going to give me a second chance?

I grasp her hands. "I know I don't deserve a second chance. But I promise if you give me one, I'll make it worth your while."

She waggles her eyebrows. "I know you will."

"Actually." I clear my throat. "I have a condition."

She yanks her hands from mine. "Excuse me? You want a second chance but you also have a condition? I don't think you understand what a second chance means."

"Can I maybe tell you the condition?" Before you stomp off and run away from me again.

She fists her hands at her hips. I'm tongue-tied for a moment at the vision. Her red hair is up in a messy bun, showing off her long, elegant neck, which I enjoy licking and biting. Her pink, pouty lips stand out against her porcelain skin. And her green eyes flash at me.

She looks good enough to eat. Which I won't be doing anytime soon.

"Go ahead. Tell me your condition."

"No sex."

She blinks several times before cleaning out her ears. "Sorry. I must have some water stuck in my ears. I think I misheard you."

"I said no sex."

"Okay. My ears aren't clogged. I'm hallucinating. Creepy crawlers in the sea. I hope I wasn't stung by a jellyfish and now I'm having some kind of psychotic episode."

I chuckle. "You didn't get stung by a jellyfish. And I'm pretty sure jellyfish stings don't cause psychotic episodes."

She grasps her chest. "There's only one explanation left. I'm dead. I've been mauled by a shark. I knew it! I always knew I'd die from a shark bite. I am haunting you until the day you die."

"You didn't get mauled by a shark. You wouldn't go out in water deeper than a foot."

She slaps a hand on my chest and I capture it. "Sharks can swim in water less than a foot deep. I know this! I've researched it."

"In which case, you also know sharks are most likely to attack in water ten to thirty feet deep."

"Why are we debating water depth when I've been killed? This is insane."

I place her hand over my heart. "You haven't been killed. Do you feel my heartbeat?"

She nods. "Yes."

"If you'd been killed, my heart would stop beating."

"Either I'm the sexiest ghost in the world or—"

"You're not dead."

"Or you're still the most charming man in the world."

"Ding. Ding. Ding. Correct answer."

She giggles. "Okay. I haven't been stung by a jellyfish or attacked by a shark. And yet I'm still pretty certain I heard you say you don't want to have sex."

"Wrong. I want to have sex. I want to have sex with you every second of the day. I can barely keep my hands off you now. You're wearing my sweatshirt and it never looked this sexy on me. I want to throw you over my shoulder and whisk you away."

Her green eyes darken until they're nearly black. "I-I-I'm confused."

"I want to have sex, but I don't think we should."

"You're serious?"

"I want to show you there's more to us than our red-hot chemistry. Do I dream about sex with you? Yes. Do I jerk off to thoughts of you? Every-damn-time."

She gasps and I use my finger to lift her chin to shut her mouth.

"You're it for me, Blaze. The entire package. Not just awesome sex but companionship as well. You make me laugh. You make me feel lighter when my mind is dark. I can tell you anything and you won't judge me. You were once my best friend. I want to be your best friend again."

"You want to be my best friend?"

"Keep up. I want to be your best friend, your lover, your everything."

Her eyes widen. "No pressure then."

"Definitely no pressure about sex since we're abstaining."

Her eyebrows raise. "We're abstaining? You made this decision for both of us?"

I blow out a breath as I tiptoe onto the tight walk set out before me. "I'm not trying to make a decision for you. I'm trying to show you how much you mean to me. How you aren't some warm body for me to use."

I palm her cheek. "You're my Blaze. You're special. And I want to show you how special you are."

"You don't realize how high the bar you're setting is."

"I don't give a fuck. I'll rent a plane to fly over the bar if I need to. I'm not giving up on you, Blaze. I will prove to you how wonderful we are together."

"Let's define this no sex rule."

My cock twitches. It didn't hear the word 'no'. It heard sex and the object of its every desire is standing in front of it. It's ready to lay her down and bury itself deep inside her.

"I don't understand." I can barely think with my cock pounding in my board shorts.

"Does no sex mean no kissing, no touching, no oral pleasure, no penetration, or all of the above?"

I inhale a deep breath and count backwards from twenty as I try to get myself under control. Judging by the twinkle in Hazel's eyes, she knows exactly how she's tempting me. My wicked temptress.

"Kissing and touching – yes. No oral pleasure and definitely no penetration."

She splays her hands over my chest before drawing them down. "I can touch here?"

I stop her before she reaches my shorts. "No touching below the belt."

She giggles. "Are we back in high school?"

"If we're back in high school, then there's only one thing to say."

"Which is?"

I repeat the question I asked her when I was a pimple-faced teenager. "Hazel Harris, will you go out on a date with me?"

She bites her bottom lip. "I don't know, Miles Raider. You have a reputation."

"Come on. You can handle a boy with a reputation."

Her eyes flash. "Of course, I can."

"Good. Because we're going out on a date tomorrow. Be ready by six. I'll pick you up."

I kiss her nose before walking away to my car. I'm not giving her a chance to change her mind. And if she's not at home tomorrow, I'll search the entire island until I find her.

This is my second chance and I'm not screwing it up.

Chapter 20

A loophole isn't cheating.

Hazel

I pace in front of the living room window as I wait for Miles to show up. Am I making a mistake?

I am. This is a bad idea. Miles isn't trustworthy. He's going to hurt me and then, when my heart is bleeding from being torn into shreds by him, he's going to throw me in the ocean for the sharks to fight over.

I must have been temporarily out of my mind yesterday to agree to give Miles a second chance. I blame those stupid blonde college students. If he hadn't ignored them in favor of spending time with me, I could have kept my walls up. Add in his proclamation that he hasn't had sex for a year with anyone else but me and my walls didn't melt. They blew to smithereens.

I should rebuild those walls before he arrives. I should encase my heart in steel and hide it behind those walls. I should—

The doorbell rings.

The time for 'I should' has passed.

I inhale a deep breath, smooth a hand down my blouse, and force my legs to the front door.

"Hi." It's the only word I can manage to get out. Holy smugglers fleeing from the Prohis. Miles is one handsome man in a dark blue button-down shirt with the sleeves rolled up, showcasing the roped muscles in his forearms.

"You look gorgeous." He kisses my cheek before handing me a bouquet of daisies. "These are for you."

I lift an eyebrow. "You remembered my favorite flower?"

"How could I forget when you had a knock-down-drag-out fight with the biology teacher over whether a daisy is a flower or a composite flower head? I don't even know what those words mean, but I remember the screeching match."

I sniff. "I did not screech at Mr. Ulrich."

"And you didn't get detention either."

"I can't believe I was forced to weed the flower beds in front of the school."

"You were adorable in your overalls with dirt streaked on your face."

I narrow my eyes at him. "No one is adorable in overalls."

"Disagree."

"Whatever," I mutter. "Let me put these flowers in water and then I'm ready to go."

I put the flowers in a vase on my kitchen table before returning to Miles. I motion him out the door. "Where are we going today?"

He grins. "The *Bootlegger Escape Room Festival*."

The *Bootlegger Escape Room Festival* is one of the many festivals on Smuggler's Hideaway developed to pull in tourists. The team to answer the bootlegger trivia and drink shots of moonshine faster than any other team wins. The prize is a night of drinking free at the *Rumrunner* speakeasy.

Although the festival was originally intended for tourists, the locals love it. The team from the *Five Fathoms* brewery has won two years in a row. Although, last year they tied with the Raider brothers. Speaking of the brothers…

"Don't you want to do the escape room with your brothers?"

He grasps my hand and threads his fingers through mine. "Nope. I don't need to spend any more time with my brothers. I see those assholes every day at work."

"You do? I thought you preferred surfing to showing up at work."

"Actually." He pulls on the collar of his shirt. It's a nervous tic and absolutely adorable. Miles is usually Mr. Confident. Seeing him less than confident – vulnerable even – is a gift. "I spoke to Eli."

"You listened to a suggestion from me?"

"Don't be a smart ass."

"I can't help it. This ass is smart all on its own."

His blue eyes darken until they're the color of the deepest ocean. "Your ass is something all right."

"No sex, remember?"

He groans. "I remember."

"I was teasing. I never agreed to the no sex rule."

He blows out a breath. "You're going to be the death of me."

I tilt my head back and speak to the heavens above. "And what a glorious death it shall be."

He chuckles.

"So…" I push. "What did Eli say?"

"We're going on a trip next month to speak to a distributor together. If things go well, I'll slowly take over contact with distributors and the big accounts."

"And you won't be behind your desk all the time."

"And I won't be behind my desk all the time."

"And maybe you won't resent your job as much if you can travel more."

"Don't push your luck, Blaze."

I shrug. "Sue me. I want you to be happy."

He squeezes my hand. "Thanks."

We arrive at the center of town, where the *Bootlegger Escape Room Festival* is happening. A conference room in City Hall has been turned into an escape room for the weekend. Each team gets a time slot of an hour. If you can't escape in an hour, you're automatically disqualified.

"I'm surprised you got a time slot," I say as we line up for our turn.

His cheeks darken, and I gasp. "No. You did not steal a time slot."

"Can you steal a time slot? It's not a tangible thing."

"Smugglers galore! You totally stole a time slot."

He scans the area. "Keep it down."

"How did you do it?" I whisper.

"Sorry. Proprietary secret."

I snort. "You had Jaxon do it."

He shrugs. "Jaxon said he was happy for the chance to practice his skills."

The large countdown clock above City Hall hits five minutes. Miles places his hand on my lower back and steers me toward the entrance. "Come on. We're next."

We reach the outside of the escape room, where a table is set up for participants to check in. We quickly register before taking our place in front of the entrance.

"Should we discuss strategy?" Miles asks.

"We go in. Answer the questions faster than anyone else and we win."

"What about the moonshine shots? Do you want me to drink all of them while you concentrate on answering clues?"

"You drink my shots? Why would…" I trail off with a gasp. "Now I know how the Raider brothers won last year. They cheated."

"Technically, it wasn't cheating. There's no requirement for *every* contestant to drink. Only that all of the shots must be drunk. Ask Paisley. Eli's girlfriend is the one who figured out the loophole."

"And now the women of *Five Fathoms Brewing* win every year." I frown. "Not this year. This year is my year."

"I love it when you get all bloodthirsty."

"I hate losing."

"I know, little Miss Competitive."

The light above the escape room flashes red. "Here we go."

The door opens automatically and we rush inside. I glance around the room searching for clues and my gaze falls upon an open bootlegger's notebook. "The rum is in the…"

"The chicken coop," Miles says from where he's glancing over my shoulder.

"Correct answer!" I high-five him before picking up the first shot of moonshine.

Miles points to a card laying on a side table. "Next clue."

The card has pictures of three bottles – moonshine, whiskey, and rum – on it. I read the riddle out loud.

"A smuggler walks into a bar and orders the only drink that won't get the cops suspicious. What does he order?"

Miles snorts. "It's a trick question. He orders water."

We drink our next shot. I twirl around the room searching for the next riddle. "Here!" I shout when I notice a riddle written on a card next to a lantern.

"Bootleggers couldn't text, so they used light. One flash meant danger. Two meant…?"

"Bring the booze, obviously." Miles flashes the lantern twice and it illuminates the radio on the other side of the room. I rush toward it but he shackles my wrist.

"Forgetting something?"

I grab the shot of moonshine from him and down it as quick as I can. When it doesn't burn, I know I've had too many, but I can't stop now. I'm winning the festival this year if my blood turns to moonshine.

The sign on the radio reads 'Tune to the frequency bootleggers used to warn each other about raids.'

Miles frowns. "I have no idea."

I elbow him out of the way. "Too easy."

I move the dial to the correct station – 1-9-2-0. "It's the start of Prohibition."

Miles hands me a shot as the radio plays our next clue. "To find what you seek, look where rum sleeps and secrets keep. Three taps on the barrel will open the way."

"Where rum sleeps and secrets keep." Miles searches the room.

"Hold on. Did you say your brothers were before or after us in line for the escape room?"

"After. Why?"

I smirk. "Because I have the best idea to slow them down."

"This is why I love you. You're devious." He gives me a quick, hard kiss. "Tell me the plan."

The plan? The plan is to get my heart to start beating again after he said he loved me. Slow your flipper loving roll, Miles didn't say he loves me. It was merely an expression. Nothing more. Nothing less.

I point to the radio. "This is a retro looking radio, but it's actually modern inside." I push the retro radio out of the way to reveal a Bluetooth speaker. "If we switch the input mode, it won't play the next clue."

Miles barks out a laugh. "Devious and genius. Let's do it."

I quickly switch the input mode from radio to aux. "All the teams after us are screwed."

"Which only helps if we get out of here. Where rum sleeps and secrets keep."

I make my way to a rum barrel and tap on it three times. A click sounds before the door opens. Miles grabs my hand and drags me outside.

"We did it!"

I lift an eyebrow. "Was there any doubt?"

"Not with you by my side."

He yanks on my hand and I slam into him. Before I have a chance to say oof, his lips are on mine. He kisses me as if the entire town isn't watching us. As if he's not embarrassed to be with me. As if all those years we were apart didn't happen.

My heart doesn't stand a chance against this version of Miles. But is this version of Miles the real one?

Chapter 21

Seals give great advice. Don't let anyone tell you otherwise.

Hazel

I skip up the walkway to my apartment building. I'm ridiculous, but I can't help it. Ever since Miles and I won the *Bootlegger Escape Room Festival*, I've been riding a high.

After Miles thoroughly kissed me in front of the town after we finished the escape room, he escorted me to *Rumrunner,* where Harper announced we'd won the festival. Let the drinking begin!

Miles took care of me throughout the night. He made sure I had enough water to drink, got some food in my stomach, and scared away any men who dared to glance in my direction. I haven't felt that safe and protected in years.

When the night was over, he escorted me home. He made sure I had a bottle of water and some aspirin next to my bed, kissed me goodnight, and left.

I was a bit disappointed after all the kissing and touching and heated glances all night but when Miles messaged the second he got home to tell me he was thinking of me, my disappointment disappeared in a poof of air.

I need to watch myself. I'm falling in love with Miles again and I should know better. Scratch that. I do know better.

But I can't seem to stop myself. Especially after he had Parker from *Pirate's Pastries* stop by with an extra-large coffee and a baked peaches and cream whiskey muffin the next morning. Parker usually doesn't do deliveries. Her bakery is busy enough without adding a delivery service to the mix.

My phone rings and I answer without checking who's calling. It's probably Miles.

"Hello!" I practically sing.

"Ms. Harris. This is Major Phillips calling from the VA hospital."

My heart pounds in my chest. This is good news, right? He wouldn't call to tell me I didn't get the job. Or would he?

"Major Phillips. It's nice to hear from you."

"You should call me Ed. Especially since we're going to be working together."

I gasp. "I got the job?"

"You got the job."

"Whoop!"

He chuckles. "The HR department sent you a letter with the official offer, including salary and benefits, but I wanted to let you know."

"Thank you."

"I look forward to working with you. Let me know what you think of the offer."

He rings off and I collapse on my couch. Thank the moonshine! I got the job. I can work full-time as a therapist. Bye-bye restaurant work. I won't miss you.

But I will miss this island. There's no way I can work at the VA hospital and still live on Smuggler's Hideaway. Not with all the traffic. Especially in the summer when tourists descend on the island.

This is my home. My family is here. My friends. *Miles.*

No. Nope. No way. I am not making any decisions based on a man – no matter how sexy said man is. I will decide whether to accept this job based on all kinds of factors – excluding my hormones.

What am I going to do? Accept my dream job or stay on the island? I drop my face in my hands.

I do the one thing I always do when I need to think. I grab my phone and keys and go in search of Pinkie.

I ride my bike out of the town of Smuggler's Cove. Maybe I'll ride to Rogue's Landing or to Pirate's Perch on the other side of the island. Maybe I'll ride up to *Mermaid Mystical Gardens.* Maybe I'll—

I hit my brakes and barely manage to screech to a halt before colliding with the gray lump in the middle of the road.

"Sammy!" I scold once I've managed to park my bike on the side of the road.

My hands are still shaking when I sit down next to the seal. "You're not supposed to be sleeping on the road. What if I was a car? I would have hit you."

He barks.

"I was paying attention."

He honks.

"I was!"

He grunts.

"Ugh! You're one to talk. You're barring the whole road. You can't complain about my driving skills when you're creating chaos."

He grunts.

"It's still chaos even if I'm the only person affected."

Sammy glances away – the disapproval clear in his eyes. Don't ask me how a seal can appear disappointed. But know – this one can.

"What do you think, Sammy?" I prop myself against a tree and settle in for a gab with the one man on the island who won't talk back. "Should I stay or should I go?"

Sammy meets my gaze before shuffling a bit closer. Phew. He's nearly on the shoulder. He should be safe from any cars now.

"I have a great job offer. It's at a VA hospital. I love working with veterans. They are one motivated bunch. Plus, my boss is totally cool. Wicked smart. Always informed about the latest developments in therapy. It would be a great learning experience."

He barks.

"Huh. It does sound as if I've already made up my mind."

A car screeches to a halt. I frown when Miles steps out. "What are you doing here?"

He wiggles his phone at me. "I saw you on the Sammy app."

Sammy the seal has his own app. He's a celebrity. People visit the island to go 'Sammy spotting'. You can mark sightings of Sammy in the app. Anyone who manages ten sightings in one weekend, gets free drinks at *Five Fathoms Brewing.*

"Saw me?"

"The Sammy app includes video now."

"I knew I should have voted against the mayor's idea of putting up cameras all over town."

"It's for our safety."

"And violates our privacy."

Miles grins as he sits next to me. "Violates our privacy because you don't want to get caught streaking through downtown?"

I elbow him. "I'm not the one who got caught streaking through downtown while carrying a raccoon."

"Not any old raccoon. It was Rogue from Rogue's Landing. The people of Rogue's Landing hadn't even realized I'd stolen their live mascot."

It's tradition on the island to 'steal' the live mascot from other towns. Smuggler's Rest has an otter named Viking. No one has a chance of stealing him since Parker keeps him close to her at all times. Rogue's Landing has the raccoon. And Pirate's Perch has a dirty-mouthed parrot.

"I can't believe Rogue didn't bite you."

He grins. "He likes me."

Sammy barks.

"And I like you, too, Sammy."

"You and animals. You're almost as good with them as my brothers."

"Whoa! No one is as good with animals as Thomas and Ian. Those sheep would jump off a cliff for your brothers."

"Let's hope not. Sounds bloody."

Silence falls but it doesn't last long. "You going to tell me what's wrong?"

I wasn't planning on it. "Why do you think anything's wrong?"

He motions toward my bike. "You only ride your bike when you're upset or drunk. You're not drunk. You must be upset."

"How do you know I'm not drunk? Maybe I had a boozy brunch with cocktails."

He lifts his eyebrow and waits. I blow out a breath.

"Fine. I didn't have a boozy brunch."

He nudges me with his shoulder. "What's wrong? Why are you upset? Do you need me to ruin someone's life?"

"You can ruin someone's life?"

He snorts. "Have you met my brothers?"

He's not wrong.

"Come on. Tell me what's wrong. I can't fix it if I don't know what it is."

"You don't need to fix anything. I can handle anything life throws at me."

He drops an arm around my shoulders and draws me near. "I know you can. But you don't have to. You have me now."

I wish I had him. I wish I could trust him to stay when the staying gets tough. But I can't. He's already bored with his job at the distillery. What happens when the newness of our relationship has worn off? Will his boredom chase him away from Smuggler's Hideaway again?

I push those thoughts away. I have enough on my plate without worrying about Miles.

"I got a job."

"Yes! How exciting! We should celebrate. Drinks, dinner, dancing, karaoke. The whole shebang!"

I stop him before he can jump to his feet. "It's not on the island."

He freezes. "Not on the island?"

"If I accept the job, I'm moving."

"I thought you loved this island."

"I do. I love Smuggler's Hideaway, but I can't stay here if there isn't work for me."

"What if you could find a job on the island? Would you stay?"

"Silly question. There are no jobs for me on Smuggler's Hideaway."

"You didn't answer the question."

I roll my eyes. "If a miracle occurred and a job for a physical therapist magically appeared in the Easter Bunny's basket, then, yes, I would stay."

"Okay. Good to know." He squeezes my hand. "Now, tell me all about this job."

I proceed to tell him all about my internship with the Army Medical Retention Processing Unit when I was in grad school.

How I met Major Phillips there. How I love working with military members.

I avoid any discussion of moving. Of leaving the only place I've ever considered home.

Leaving him. Miles. The only man who's ever made me feel safe. Not just physically but safe to be me.

My stomach clenches. Can I leave Miles? After I've finally given him a second chance?

Chapter 22

I don't care what anyone says. Helping your girlfriend is a kind gesture.

MILES

I stride into the *Hideaway Haven Resort.* I don't know if this idea will work, but I have to try. I can't lose Hazel. Not now, after she's finally given me a second chance.

"May I help you?" The front desk worker – Roger, according to his badge – asks.

"I'm here to see Hudson."

He frowns. "Hudson?"

"Mr. Clark," I clarify, although I'm not certain why I'm clarifying. Surely, he knows Hudson owns this resort. Everyone on the island knows who Hudson is, considering he grew up here and became a famous NFL player. When he got injured and couldn't play ball anymore, he returned to the island to start this resort.

"Do you have an appointment?"

"No. Tell him Miles is here."

"Miles?"

Roger is obviously not from the island. No Smuggler can sound as condescending as he does.

"Miles Raider, Eli Raider's little brother."

He sniffs. "You're Eli Raider's brother?"

Of course, he knows Eli's name. Eli is a billionaire. Everyone on the island knows who he is.

"My mom claims we're brothers," I joke, since Roger could use more laughter in his life.

"Yes, well, Mr. Clark is not simply available for someone's brother."

"Can you ring him and let him know I'm here?"

A smuggler never refuses to see another smuggler. Unless they're feuding. And, luckily, no one has been feuding on the island for a couple of decades.

"I will not. This is ridiculous. I have other customers to help."

I glance behind me but the reception area is empty. Other customers?

Before I can tell him he's more delusional than a pirate being sung to by a siren, the door behind him opens and Hudson walks out.

I smile. "Hudson."

"Miles Raider." He grins as he comes around the desk to shake my hand. "Haven't seen you in forever."

"Probably because you hide out in your resort with your wife and child and have abandoned the rest of the island."

"Nova and Iliana are my life."

The happiness beaming from him is infectious. I want what he has. The girl I fell in love with in high school. Children to bind us together. And I'm not stopping until I have it all.

"Why did you stop by today? To discuss how the products from *Buccaneer's Whiskey & Distillery* are doing?" He ushers me toward the bar area. "Do you have any new products? The Christmas moonshine Jaxon developed was incredibly popular. I bet a summer moonshine would do well, too."

"I'll let Jaxon know."

Unlike me, who failed to make a new flavor in a bid to impress Hazel, Jaxon, as the master distiller, develops popular new flavors all the time.

"Here." Hudson scoots behind the bar. "Let me make a print-out of our most popular drinks and how much we use *Buccaneer's*."

I start to stop him but pause. This is my job as sales manager for the distillery. I should probably visit big clients more often. Get out of the office and away from my hated desk. The way Hazel suggested.

We find a table in the rear of the bar. Hudson and I review the popular summer drinks and how they could use a Buccaneer's product in most of them. By the time we finish, the purchase order from the resort has nearly doubled.

"This has been a productive meeting," Hudson says as he stands.

"Um, there is one more thing I need to discuss."

His brow wrinkles. "Please don't tell me *Buccaneer's* is developing some crazy adventure sport circuit. Zane has been pushing me on the topic for years."

"You have no need to worry. Zane's calmed down since he became a dad."

Hudson shakes his head as he sits back down. "I can't believe a woman left a baby on his doorstep."

I raise an eyebrow. "You can't?"

He barks out a laugh. "Okay, it's Zane. I can."

"Anyway." I clear my throat. "I wanted to ask you about your physical therapist."

He scowls. "What physical therapist? I couldn't find anyone willing to relocate to the island. I promised the coach I'd have a therapist when training camp starts."

"Coach? Training camp?"

"Crap." He rubs a hand down his face. "I'm trying to keep the arrival of the team's stay here a secret but judging by the smile on your face, you already know."

I shrug. "There have been rumors."

"This town."

"Don't worry. No smuggler will speak to a tourist about it, and they'll drive all the journalists off the cliff."

He laughs. "Maybe we shouldn't discuss murdering journalists. It's frowned upon."

"Okay. Let's discuss the physical therapist."

"The person who doesn't exist."

"But she does."

His brow wrinkles. "She does?"

"Hazel Harris."

I hold my breath as Hudson considers. "Hazel wants the job? What about the whole 'I work for myself. No one else'?"

I never heard Hazel say those words, but I wouldn't be surprised if she did. She is the most stubborn woman I know.

"She's considering a job at a VA hospital."

"VA hospital? There isn't one close. She'd have to..." Hudson frowns at me. "You don't want her to move."

"It's stupid of her to move when the perfect job is right here. Assuming you would hire her."

He scoffs. "Of course, I'd hire Hazel. She did an awesome job getting Caleb back into shape. But she hasn't applied for the position."

"Could you offer her the job anyway?"

He leans forward on his elbows and meets my gaze. "What's happening here?"

"I don't want Hazel to move away. She's finally given me a second chance and I don't want to lose her."

"She's given you a second chance?"

I blow out a breath. "Don't act as if you don't know. You're not the hermit you once were. Nova is a proud member of the gossip brigade."

"Fine. I'll skip over the teasing and get to the heart of the matter. You want me to give your girlfriend a job?"

My nose wrinkles. "Why do you sound disgusted by the idea?"

"Because it's stupid."

"Stupid? This is a grand gesture to show her how much I love her. How much I'll miss her if she leaves the island."

"You forgot how much you want to control her."

"I don't want to control Hazel."

He snorts. "No? You aren't controlling where she'll live and where she'll work?"

I blow out a breath. This conversation is not going the way I expected it to.

"I don't understand what the problem is. You need a physical therapist. You would love to hire Hazel. What's the problem?"

"No problem for me. I'll speak to Hazel and offer her the job. You may want to hide for a few days, though."

"You're exaggerating."

"And you don't understand relationships."

"Hudson!" Roger bustles toward us. "I'm sorry to interrupt." He smiles at me as if he is actually apologetic. "But there's an emergency with one of the rooms."

Hudson stands with a sigh. "I bet I know what kind of emergency. You'd be amazed how many women lock themselves out of their rooms while they're naked."

"I won't tell Nova."

"She probably already knows. I think she has my resort bugged."

I chuckle as he walks away. I stand to go back to work but then I remember – the purchase order. Can't forget it. Talk about a successful meeting. Hudson agreed to buy more whiskey and moonshine from *Buccaneer's,* and he's going to offer Hazel a job.

My Blaze won't have to leave the island – giving me time to win her over and prove she was right to give me a second chance. I can't wait for our life together to begin.

Chapter 23

A second chance doesn't mean go ahead and trample all over my life.

Hazel

I tap the envelope with my finger. It's a thick envelope containing the VA hospital's job offer. Is it a good offer? No idea. I haven't opened it yet.

What if it's a great offer? I can't turn down a great offer. Even if it means leaving home.

Ugh! I hate being indecisive. Usually, I can make a decision within minutes. But this decision has me torn in two.

My phone rings and I snatch at the opportunity to take my mind off this job offer.

"Hello."

"Hazel?"

The voice sounds familiar, but I can't place it. "This is Hazel. Who am I speaking to?"

"Hudson."

Of course, I know Hudson. He owns the *Hideaway Haven Resort*. He's also a local celebrity who used to play in the NFL. Plus, he grew up on the island.

"Oh, hi, Hudson. How are you? How are Nova and Iliana?"

"I'm good, and they're perfect."

I sigh. Nova is the luckiest girl on the island. To have a big, strong football player who lived as a hermit fight his demons for you? Swoon!

"I'm glad. Why are you calling me?"

He chuckles. "Always to the point."

"I can beat around the bush for a while if you prefer. But you're a busy man."

"I am. I'll get to the point then. I want to hire you."

"Hire me? I don't remember applying for a job."

"I don't need to interview you. I know you're an excellent physical therapist. And I need a physical therapist."

"You just happened to remember I'm a physical therapist?"

"I might have been reminded by someone."

I swear under my breath. "Miles set me up. I'm going to whip him with his surfboard."

"In his defense, I wouldn't offer you the job if I didn't think you were capable."

"You're seriously offering me this job? It's not a pity ask?"

"Not sure what a pity ask is, but I'm offering you the job. It would be full-time, and you'd also be on call for weekends and holidays. You can bring your own clients with you and maintain your current payment arrangement with them. The resort would earn no money on those clients."

Holy smugglers. This sounds perfect. I could stay on the island and still work as a therapist.

"Miles might have reminded me you're a therapist, but I should have offered you the job before."

"I need to think about it." And go find Miles so I can give him a piece of my mind.

"Take your time. And don't hurt him too bad."

He rings off and I shove my phone in my pocket before grabbing my keys. Miles better hope I can't find him because I am not a happy mermaid.

I stomp out of my apartment, but once I reach the sidewalk, I pause. I have no idea where Miles is. But I have an ace in the hole. Someone who can't refuse to answer me after what she did.

Harper answers on the first ring. "Hey, Hazel. Where are you? Are you coming?"

"Coming where?"

"*Mermaid Mini Golf.* The whole family is here."

"The whole family?"

"If you're asking whether Miles is here, he is. If you hurry, you can be on his team. Dad, don't touch that. Sorry, I need to go before Dad destroys a mermaid."

When we hang up, I check my phone. No messages from Miles inviting me to a family event. Great. Mr. Hot and Cold has arrived at the party. This is why I didn't want to give him a chance. I can't trust him to always be there.

Like now. He's switched off again. But why? Why arrange a job for me and then switch off? Miles Raider is the most confusing man I've ever met.

He's also the man who will be answering all my questions. As soon as I can make it to *Mermaid Mini Golf.*

I jump in my car and drive as fast as possible toward the cliffs. On one side is *Mermaid Mystical Gardens.* On the other side is *Mermaid Mini Golf.* In between is a statue of a poor mermaid who believed a smuggler when he claimed he loved her and ended up diving to her death off the cliffs.

The Raider family has taken over the mini golf course. There are Raiders everywhere. Pearl is running around the giant mermaid at the fifth hole while Rhett chases her. Dakota is sitting on a bench with baby Mira, laughing.

"Miles Raider!" I stomp toward where he's standing with Jaxon and Sloane, waiting for their turn to begin.

"It's about time you got here," Jaxon says. "We're about to start."

"You were expecting me? Odd since I wasn't invited."

Miles holds up his hands. "I didn't invite you because you're supposed to be working at *Smuggler's Cove Restaurant* tonight."

I narrow my eyes at him. "How do you know when I'm supposed to work?"

He shakes his phone at me. "I have your schedule synced to mine."

"You have…" I shake my head. Miles knowing my schedule is not the issue here. His not inviting me tonight isn't either. Although, I'm happy to hear he didn't forget all about me.

Maybe Mr. Hot and Cold hasn't returned to the party yet after all.

"Did you speak to Hudson?"

His cheeks darken. "Y-y-yes."

"How dare you ask him to offer me a pity job!"

"Can we discuss this somewhere private?" He motions to his brothers, who have given up on mini golf and are inching their way toward us.

"What's a pity job?" Sloane asks.

"Please. Somewhere private," Miles pleads.

I snort. "First of all, there's nowhere private enough on this island to keep your family from eavesdropping."

"Not fair," Zane claims while he rocks Adele in his arms. "I don't eavesdrop when it's adult time."

Pearl tugs on his jeans. "What's adult time? Mom and Dad take naps during adult time. But I'm not allowed to join them."

"Pearl." Rhett rushes to pick her up while Dakota's cheeks darken until they're bright red.

I ignore all of them to glare at Miles. "Did you or did you not ask Hudson to give me a pity job?"

"It's not a fucking pity job," he grumbles.

"Swear jar, Uncle Miles!"

Rhett covers Pearl's mouth with his hand. "Sorry."

Henry, Harper's dad, wheels his way toward us. "What's going on? I was promised a burger and fries."

Harper glares at Kai. "Who promised you a burger and fries?"

"It won't kill him to eat a burger and fries once in a while."

Harper throws her arms in the air. "I give up!"

"If you're done discussing what I'm allowed to eat, can someone tell me what the holdup is?" Henry asks.

I point to Miles. "He went behind my back to get me a job at the resort."

"I didn't go behind your back."

I spit daggers out of my eyes at him. "Did you tell me what you were doing? No. You did not. You snuck off to speak to Hudson about me." I slam a hand on my chest. "About my career without consulting me."

"I wanted to give you options."

"I can't believe you. You ignore me for years."

He growls. "I never ignored you."

He so did. I get all up in his face. As much as is possible, considering I'm several inches shorter than him.

"You ignored me for years except when you were drunk and horny. And when I'm finally getting my career on track and have an awesome job opportunity with a VA hospital, you decide you can't handle it and stick your big, fat nose in my business."

"I do not have a fat nose."

I growl. His nose is not the point and he knows it!

"Never mind my nose," he quickly backpedals. "You told me you would stay on Smuggler's Hideaway if you had a job here."

"So you went and got me a job."

"I don't want you to leave."

"I don't care!"

"Yes, you do," he grumbles. "You don't want to move away from Smuggler's Hideaway. You want to stay. What's the big deal? Hudson wouldn't hire you if he didn't think you could do the job. He was impressed with how you treated Caleb."

"None of this is the point." I stab him in the chest. He tries to capture my hand but I step backwards before he has the chance. "You can't control me. This is my life. My career. I make the decisions. Not you."

He reaches for me. "I'm not trying to control you."

I bat him away. "I'm done here." I whirl around and march toward my car.

"This isn't the end," Miles hollers after me. "You can be mad at me and stomp away, but this isn't us breaking up. We're having a fight. We're not ending. We're never ending."

How I wish I could believe him. But he pushed a job on me after less than a week of dating. How is he going to try to control me after a year? A decade?

Can I ever trust him again?

Chapter 24

When you have five brothers, there is no such thing as quiet time.

Miles

I stride out of the water carrying my surfboard. I've been out here surfing for hours. Trying to find some peace and calm. Wondering how I could screw up so thoroughly with Hazel within a week of her giving me a second chance.

Should I walk away now? Let Hazel go find a man who isn't a screw-up. A man who has more experience with relationships.

I don't want to walk away. I know in my heart that Hazel is the one for me. I've always known it. From the first time she laughed at me in biology class freshman year.

But if I can't make her happy, maybe I should let her go. I want to throw up at the thought. If Hazel isn't in my life, I'll have a big hole in my chest until my last moment on earth.

I start toward my shack. I need to put away my board and get showered before I go into the office.

I slow when I realize there are five men sitting on the sand in front of my shack. Damnit. I was hoping to avoid this. And by this, I mean my brothers being all up in my business.

I prop my board in the sand and sit down. "Let's get this over with."

"Over with?" Jaxon pushes his glasses up his face. "We're here to offer our support. Not interrogate you."

"Speak for yourself," Kai mutters. "I'm here to give him a piece of my mind. My fiancé is pissed. She wants Hazel for a sister, but you screwed it all up."

I scowl at him. "Hazel and I aren't broken up."

Zane raises his eyebrow. "You aren't?"

"No. Two people can fight without breaking up. We'll fix this."

"Good." Eli nods. "You're maturing. This makes me feel better about including you on the trip to visit the *Velvet Blossom* headquarters. The restaurant chain is one of our biggest accounts."

"And, congrats, on the extra-large purchase order from Hudson," Rhett adds.

Despite how shitty I'm feeling, I can't help but smile at the pride in Eli and Rhett's voices. Those two gave up their teenage years to take care of us younger brothers. It feels good to make them proud.

"I should have visited Hudson earlier. We tweaked his bar menu. Now all of the popular cocktails include spirits from *Buccaneer's*."

Kai holds up his hand. "Hold on. Hold on. Hold on. Is Miles seriously discussing work when he doesn't have to? Jaxon, you're closest. Check if he has a fever."

Jaxon wrinkles his nose. "You do realize placing a hand over someone's forehead is not an accurate means to check their temperature?"

"Hold on. I might have a thermometer with me." Zane digs through his bag. "It's probably a rectal one."

Kai chuckles. "How do we decide who gets to stick it up Miles's ass?"

I growl. "No one is sticking a thermometer up my ass."

He motions to Jaxon. "But he said we needed a thermometer."

"I did not..." Jaxon sighs. "Whatever. Can we get this meeting over with? Some of us have jobs to do."

"Does it bother you how Jaxon thinks he's busier than you?" I ask Eli. "You're the CEO of the distillery and you're also the CFO of *Apparoo*."

Apparoo is the company Eli founded with his college roommate, Jeremy. Its success is why he's a billionaire. And now the company is relocating to Smuggler's Hideaway since Jeremy fell in love with the local bakery owner, Parker.

Eli smirks. "Your lame attempt to change the subject is what bothers me."

I blow out a breath. "What's the subject? How awesome I am at my job? I'm willing to spend some time discussing this."

Zane's jaw drops open. "Is Miles talking about working in an office? A place he professes to hate?"

I wag a finger at him. "You're one to talk. Until baby Adele came into your life, you skipped out on work more often than I did."

Zane was actually packing for a motorcycle trip through South America when Adele was dropped on his doorstep. Literally, a woman stopped by, said the baby was his, dropped her on his porch, and left.

He points to Kai. "He was just as bad about missing work."

Kai waggles his eyebrows. "I needed the love of a good woman to settle me down."

I snort. "And Harper won't put up with your childish ways."

"You say…"

I ignore him when I feel something scuttle up my leg. I jump to my feet and a sand crab falls out of my board shorts before scurrying away.

"Who put the animal up my leg?"

"Congrats, brother. Even the wildlife's running from your love life."

I dive at Kai, but before I can pummel him, Rhett pushes us apart.

"Epic prank!"

I glare at Kai. "Pranks aren't supposed cause bodily harm."

"Sand crabs don't bite."

I motion to the small, red bumps on my ankle. "It wasn't a sand crab, you idiot. It was a sand flea."

"Oops!"

I dive for Kai again but Rhett shoves me. "Knock it off. It's not as if you've never pulled a prank that resulted in bodily harm before."

I cross my arms over my chest. "Name one time."

"When Ms. Milton broke her ankle."

"It's not my fault she ran away when the skeleton appeared."

"When Weston crashed his car."

"Again, not my fault. He thought he saw an animal in the road."

"Because you planted a fake shark in the middle of the road.

I shrug. "He should be more careful."

Rhett throws his arms in the air. "I can't with you and the pranks."

Jaxon stands and brushes the sand off his clothes. He's wearing his standard uniform of jeans and a dorky t-shirt. This one says *Never trust an atom. They make up everything.*

"If we're not discussing Miles's problem, I'm returning to the distillery."

Kai rubs his hands together. "Are you mixing flavors? Do you have samples?"

Zane shakes his head. "Once you get Harper pregnant, it'll be the end of day drinking for you."

"Goodbye." Jaxon walks off but Eli calls him back. "Time to discuss Miles's problem."

"I don't have a problem."

Rhett smirks. "You arranged a job for Hazel."

Zane chuckles. "Who's even more stubborn than Sloane."

"She got a job offer at a VA hospital. She was thinking about moving. I panicked."

"And took things into your own hands without discussing it with her?" Eli asks.

"You make it sound bad."

"Because it is. She thinks you're trying to control her."

I scowl. "I don't want to control her. Her fire is one of the things I adore about her."

I love how Hazel doesn't take shit from me. She would never let me control her. Witness yesterday's display of how she responds when she thinks I am controlling her. Not a pretty sight.

"You need to explain all of this to her before she leaves the island."

Leaves the island? I clutch my chest as my heart rams against my ribcage. Is Hazel leaving already? Without saying goodbye?

"When is she leaving?" I ask Kai.

He shrugs. "No idea but Harper said she was selling her furniture."

Selling her furniture? This is serious.

I set off for the parking lot.

"You left your board out!" Eli shouts after me.

"You have keys to the shack."

All of my brothers have keys to the shack. Although, none of them surf. I should be so lucky. But they enjoy using the shower after a day on the beach. Or stealing my beer from the refrigerator on a hot summer's day.

"Does this mean I have permission to raid your supply?" Kai yells.

I flick my hand. He can do whatever he wants. I don't care about some chocolate bars and potato chips now. I have more important things to do.

As in stop the woman I love from leaving before we straighten things out. And, maybe, just maybe, stop her from leaving altogether. A man can hope.

Chapter 25

He's not supposed to remember where I keep my vases.

*H*AZEL

I flip the envelope over a few times.

"This is ridiculous," I mutter as I tear it open. "I deserve to know what the offer is."

"Dear Ms. Harris, We're excited to offer you the position of Physical Therapist. Yada yada yada. Your annual salary will consist of…"

I gasp and drop the envelope. I must be seeing things. Maybe I need glasses. No way, no how are they offering me *that* salary. Plus four weeks paid vacation, health care, and a retirement plan. This isn't a good offer. It's a great offer.

It could be the dawn of a new career for me. I could travel from VA hospital to VA hospital across the country.

My stomach sours. Instead of being away from Smuggler's Hideaway for a few years, I'd be gone my entire career.

This is the truth I didn't want to admit to myself. If I leave the island to become a PT somewhere else, I can't come back in a year or two. It's not as if the inhabitants of this island will grow. And once I'm gone, it'll be easier to stay away.

The doorbell rings. I stuff the offer back in the envelope and shove it in a kitchen drawer before going to answer the bell.

"Miles. How did you know I'd be home?"

He kisses my cheek before handing me a bouquet of daisies and a card. "You usually don't work on Sunday nights since you have therapy patients on Monday morning."

"Have you been stalking me?"

He barks out a laugh. "I'm stalking you because I know your routine?"

"You also synced my schedule to your agenda."

He shrugs. "Did you forget we live on Smuggler's Hideaway?"

"I might not live here for long."

The words taste like acid in my mouth, but they're true.

"Can I come in?"

I open the door wide to allow him inside.

"Shall I put these in a vase?" he asks but doesn't wait for a response. He marches straight to my kitchen and opens the cabinet holding the vases.

"Now I know you're stalking me."

He glances up from pouring water into the vase to smile at me. His blue eyes twinkle with amusement. "Why?"

I point to the vase. "How else did you know where my vases are?"

"It's the cabinet they were in the last time I brought you flowers."

"And you remembered?"

"I remember everything about you. Every second we've spent together."

I snort. "Pretty sure you don't remember senior skip day when you drank a bottle of moonshine before riding *Siren's Spiral* at *Mermaid Mystical Gardens.*"

"Correction. I remember almost every second we've spent together."

"I wish I didn't remember senior skip day. Vomiting is not attractive."

Miles shrugs. "We were stupid kids."

I lift an eyebrow. "And you're not stupid anymore?"

He sighs before putting the vase of daisies on my kitchen table. "I'm sorry. I shouldn't have spoken to Hudson about a job for you without telling you in advance."

I clear my throat. "Try again."

"I shouldn't have spoken to Hudson about a job for you, full stop?"

"Ding! Ding! Ding! Correct answer."

"Can we sit down and discuss this?"

"I don't know what there is to discuss. You tried controlling me. I didn't enjoy it."

He grasps my hand and leads me to the living room, where we settle on the couch next to each other. Despite the inches between us, I can feel the heat radiating off him. Miles always did run hotter than normal. Probably a good thing considering his love for surfing in the ocean all year round.

Miles squeezes my hand. "I truly am sorry. I panicked."

"You panicked?"

He blows out a breath. "The thought of you not living on this island…Of not being near me. Of not bumping into you at the restaurant or bar. It unravels me."

How long have I waited for Miles to talk this way? To admit the effect I have on him? To not run away from me and his feelings for me?

No matter how long I've waited, I can't let him control my life and my career.

"Causing you to lose control of your actions?"

"Causing me to become a first-class idiot who should have told you how worried he was instead of getting all sneaky."

I sigh. "I used to enjoy it when you were sneaky."

He smirks. "When we were in high school and we'd sneak into the biology lab after school to spend time together where the librarian couldn't find us?"

I slap his stomach. "You were always mean to the librarian."

"She told me I'd never amount to much!"

"Because you never finished your homework."

"I did, too! Just not at the library."

"You were too busy distracting me."

He waggles his eyebrows. "I never heard you complaining."

Of course not! I'm not an idiot. The times I fooled around with Miles in the library stacks are some of my best memories from high school.

His blue eyes heat and he leans toward me. I hold up a hand. "Slow your mermaid loving mind. We're not done discussing how you tried to control my life."

"I promise not to try and control you again."

"What happens the next time you panic?"

He shrugs. "I can't predict the future. I can promise I won't go running off and try to control your life without involving you."

"Let's test this theory." I stand.

"Where are you going?"

"Hold on a sec." I retrieve the envelope with the offer from the VA before returning and throwing it on Miles's lap.

"What's this?"

"Read it."

"It's your personal mail."

"As if respecting someone's privacy has ever stopped you before. You're still on Cora's blacklist. She will never forgive you for rifling through the letters in her postbag."

"You are giving me permission to open this?" I nod and he opens the envelope.

My knee bounces as I watch him read the letter. I study his face but he doesn't give anything away. No panic. No surprise. No happiness.

"Since when do you have a poker face?"

"Since I lost a poker game to Zane and he forced me to babysit Adele. I don't know what they feed that baby but her diapers are nasty."

I tap the letter. "What do you think?"

He smiles. "I think this is a wonderful opportunity for you."

"And?" Where's the panic?

"And I don't know what Hudson offered you, but it's going to be hard to beat this. Especially since you said you really enjoy working with military members."

"I'll have to move."

"Make sure you get an apartment with a big enough bedroom for a king-sized bed."

My brow wrinkles. "What?"

He motions to himself. "I'm too tall to sleep on a smaller bed."

"You sleep on the bed?"

"Yeah." He tugs on one of my curls. "When I visit every weekend."

"Every weekend?"

"And holidays. Although, I'll be travelling for work more often. I may have to skip a weekend here or there."

"You're serious. You would drive to the mainland to visit me every weekend?"

"I'm dead serious."

"But you won't have time to surf. What about your surfing lessons?"

"None of it matters."

My head rears back. "Excuse me. I'm hallucinating again. Did you say surfing doesn't matter? Do I need to find my thermometer to take your temperature?"

"As long as it's not a rectal thermometer," he mutters before clearing his throat. "Surfing is a sport I enjoy. It's not my life. You are."

"What?"

He throws the letter onto the coffee table before grasping my hands. "Hazel Harris, you are what matters. I love you. I've always loved you. I'll never stop loving you."

I gaze into his eyes but there's no hint of deception. It's all honesty with a hint of heat.

These are the words I've longed to hear from Miles for years. The words I dreamed he'd say when he returned home all those years ago. Instead, he ignored me most of the time. I want to reach for him. I want to believe him. But I don't know if I can.

Miles tugs on my hands until I'm forced to straddle him. He palms my face. "I don't expect you to say the words back to me. I need to show you they're true. I need to prove to you I'm here to stay. I won't run away."

I snarl. "Will you stop saying the perfect words?"

"Nope." He kisses my nose. "I will spend the rest of my life searching for the perfect words to tell you how much you mean to me."

"Miles."

"Shush now. Let me show you how I feel."

He melds his lips to mine and I gasp. He seizes the opportunity to thrust his tongue into my mouth. His wild, ocean taste hits me and I forget all about being cautious. Forget all about my fears, he'll abandon me.

Forget everything but how he tastes and how he makes me feel.

Chapter 26

It's not my fault Hazel is impossible to resist.

MILES

I growl before deepening the kiss. I angle Hazel's head to give me more room to maneuver. I love how she tastes. I could spend the day with her in my arms, tasting her.

She wiggles in my lap and my cock takes notice. It hardens and lengthens at the feel of her grinding against me.

How I want to sink deep inside her until I don't know where I end and she begins. Until all the worry I've carried for the past days disappears. Until all I know is the beauty and passion of the woman I love.

But I can't. I promised her no sex. I promised her I'd show her there's more to us than the passion we share.

"Blaze," I growl as I tear my mouth from hers. "Stop."

"Stop what?" She grinds down on my cock. "This?" She nibbles along my jaw. "Or this?"

"Blaze."

She bats her eyelashes. "What? Why are you being Mr. Grumpy? I can feel how much you're enjoying yourself."

She grinds down on my cock again and I nearly say fuck it. But I can't. I made a promise to her and if she's ever going to fall back in love with me, she needs to know she can rely on me. That I'll keep my promises to her.

"Blaze, we agreed to not have sex yet."

"Nuh-uh." She wags a finger at me. "I never agreed."

"I'm trying to show you there's more to us than our red-hot chemistry."

My resolve is quickly disintegrating with every swirl of her hips and touch of her skin against mine. I need to hold strong. But how? I've never been any good at denying myself what I want. And I want Hazel more than anything in the world.

She giggles. "You brought me daisies. You know where I keep my vases. You haven't had sex with anyone else in a year. You are going to visit me every weekend on the mainland. And you love me. We're good."

"But I tried to control you. I asked Hudson to give you a job."

"I know." She sighs. "But did you learn from your mistake?"

I nod. "I did. Don't control Hazel."

She grins. "Correct answer." She nibbles on my earlobe. "Now, are you going to make love to me, or am I going to have to kick you out of the house so I can take care of matters on my own?"

I growl. "I'll take care of you. But we will revisit you taking matters into your own hands at another time."

She giggles. "Such a man."

"A man who loves you and don't you forget it."

She gazes into my eyes as if she's searching for the truth. She can search all she wants because there is only one truth. I love her, and I'm never letting her go.

She swallows. "Okay."

Disappointment slams into me. I want her to admit her feelings for me. But I need to be patient. I was a dick to her for years after I returned home injured from my first pro surfing event. She needs time to accept I'm no longer that man.

I stand with her in my arms and carry her bridal style to her bedroom. I don't throw her on the bed the way I usually do. Nothing about today will be our usual way of doing things. We're slowing things down so I can show her how I feel.

I lay her on the bed and crawl on top of her. "You sure about this?"

She fiddles with my t-shirt. "Are you sure you won't disappear tomorrow morning?"

"I plan to stay glued to you for every moment you're on the island."

"What if I never leave?"

"Then, I'm never leaving your side."

"You better not expect me to surf by your side because sharks…" She shivers.

I kiss her nose. "The mermaids and smugglers keep the sharks at bay."

She rolls her eyes. "Whatever. I'm not learning to surf."

This is an argument we've had too many times to count. When I was young and dumb, I wanted to share my love of surfing with her. I'm not young and dumb anymore. And I refuse to argue with her about this.

Especially when I'm laying on top of her in her bed. My cock pressing hard against my zipper, impatient to sink deep inside heaven.

"I won't disappear on you again." I nibble along her jaw and she arches her neck to give me better access. "Tomorrow morning, you're going to wake up to me in this bed with you. The place I want to be forever."

She studies me for a moment before nodding. "Okay."

"Anything else you want to get off your chest before I strip you naked and give you a few orgasms?"

She taps her cheek. "Let me think. We could try to solve world hunger."

I tickle her ribs. She tries to bat me away but I'm draped over her. She doesn't stand a chance.

"Stop, Miles. I'll pee my pants."

"You can't pee your pants if you're not wearing any." I unsnap her jeans and her eyes flare. "You want to stop at any time, say the word and I'll stop."

"When have I ever wanted you to stop?"

"The time we were on the beach and you were convinced a sand crab was aiming for your pussy."

She slaps me. "I spent days getting sand out of places sand should never be in."

I don't remind her having sex on the beach was her idea. I'm not a stupid man.

"Lucky for you, there's no sand in this bed."

I draw her zipper down, exposing her pink, lace panties. As sexy as they are, they've got to go. I tap her hip and she immediately lifts up. I drag her jeans and panties down her legs and throw them over my shoulder.

I glide my fingers along her legs until I reach her core. Goosebumps follow in my wake. I love how her body responds to mine. As if her body yearns for mine. As if she can't wait for me to touch her.

"Do you want my mouth or my fingers?"

Her breath hitches. "You forgot one option."

"Don't worry, Blaze. You'll get my cock. But first I'm going to make you come with my mouth or my fingers."

"I don't recall being given a choice before."

Probably because I'm usually in a hurry to bury myself deep inside her before she runs away from me again. But I'm not worried about her running away. If she runs, I'll chase her. Hazel Harris is the only woman I'll ever love. And I'm not letting her go.

"You won't be given a choice again if you can't make up your mind."

"Mouth," she blurts out.

"Spread your legs." She doesn't hesitate to follow orders. Probably because she knows how good I can make her feel.

I lay down and fit my shoulders between her thighs. I use my fingers to open her to me. She gasps and arches off the bed.

I place an arm over her stomach. "Be still."

"You make it…" She trails off with a groan when I latch onto her clit and suck.

As much as I want to slow things down and show Hazel how much I love her, the second her taste hits my mouth, I'm lost. It's been too long since I've tasted her. I want to gorge myself on her taste.

While my tongue plays with her clit, I sink one finger into her pussy.

"Holy mermaids," she mutters as her walls flutter around my finger.

"Not a mermaid. Miles."

"Miles," she moans as I plunge two fingers into her.

I pump my fingers in and out of her while I nibble and tease her clit until she's chanting my name. "Miles. Miles. Miles."

Her walls tighten around my fingers. She's close. Thank fuck. My cock is begging to be let free. To sink into Hazel. I can feel pre-cum weeping from the tip.

"Say my name when you come."

"I'm not… I mean, I am…" She trails off when I suck her clit into my mouth.

"Miles!" she shouts as her climax hits her.

I continue to glide my fingers inside her until she collapses on the bed. I remove my fingers and gaze into her eyes as I lick them. "Mmm… delicious."

Her eyes flare and she reaches for me. I realize she's still wearing her t-shirt. This won't do. I grasp the hem and tug upwards until she raises her arms for me. I throw her t-shirt over my shoulder before ridding her of her bra.

Once she's deliciously naked, I rake my gaze over her. Her breasts are perky with pretty pink nipples. Her waist is narrow while her hips flare. She has all the curves in all the right places and I'm the lucky bastard who gets to touch her.

"I love these freckles," I murmur as I trace the little brown dots that trail from her neck to her creamy white breasts.

"Lucky you. They multiply in the summer."

"I can't wait for summer. You in a bikini at the beach. You in a wet bikini. Your bikini on the floor of my bedroom."

She giggles. "You're obsessed with my bikini."

"Wrong. I'm obsessed with you. Everything about you. From the smattering of freckles on your chest to how freaking strong you are when you help patients, to how smart you are. You, Hazel Harris, are the love of my life. I love you."

She sighs. "Someone is being Mr. Romantic today." She motions to my jeans. "Now remove your clothes and show me how you can be Mr. Pound Me Into The Mattress."

"You want me to pound you into the mattress?"

"And give me another orgasm."

"Don't you worry. I'll give you at least one more."

She lifts her eyebrows. "Two?"

"Challenge accepted."

I roll off the bed and shove my jeans down my legs before removing my shirt. Once I'm naked, I crawl back on the bed but swear and stop before I reach her.

"What's wrong?"

"Forgot a condom."

She meets my gaze. "You seriously haven't had sex with anyone but me in a year?"

"You're the only woman for me."

She widens her legs. "Then, let's forgo the condoms. I'm on the pill."

I know she's on the pill. But even if she wasn't, I wouldn't care. A baby would be a perfect way to connect us forever. I mentally slap myself. There I go again, trying to control her.

As much as I can't wait to see her stomach round with my child, the decision has to be hers. I learned my lesson. Trying to control Hazel is a one-way street to Lonely Town.

I climb back onto the bed and crawl between her legs. I notch my cock at her entrance. "You're sure?"

She digs her fingernails into my shoulders. "I'm sure."

I sink into her until my balls slap against her ass. I have to pause to get myself under control. I'm not coming like some one pump wonder just because I finally have the woman I want beneath me.

This is it. This is the woman I'm going to spend the rest of my days with. Now it's time to show her how much she means to me.

Chapter 27

I should have realized people would start betting.

Hazel

I cuddle into the warm body behind me before sighing in contentment. Last night was amazing. I should have known. Miles is right. Our chemistry is red hot.

But there's more to us than chemistry. Such as Miles cuddled into my back with his arm wrapped around my waist. And Miles saying I love you. More than once.

A tiny flicker of hope tries to ignite. I expunge it. It's too early to feel hopeful. Yes, Miles said he loves me. But he's said those words before. And then abandoned me when he started his pro surfing career. I don't trust him.

Yet.

Fine. I snarl at the overly optimistic voice in my mind. I don't trust him yet.

The flicker of hope ignites again. But I can't expunge it this time. I want to be hopeful. I want Miles to stay with me.

I love him after all. I always have. And I probably always will.

But love isn't always enough.

Miles squeezes my waist. "What are you thinking so hard about this morning?"

"How do you know I'm thinking hard?"

He rolls me onto my back before looming over me. "This tells me you're worried." He traces a finger down the wrinkle on my forehead.

"If you say I have wrinkles, I'm kicking you in the balls."

"You don't have wrinkles. But even if you did, you'd be beautiful."

I roll my eyes. "You're laying it on pretty thick this morning."

He shrugs. "I'm in a good mood. I woke up holding the woman I love in my arms."

My heart spasms the same way it always does when he says he loves me. The words cause warmth to spread throughout my body until I'm all warm and mushy.

"You don't believe me yet. But you will." He kisses my nose before hopping out of bed. "What do you want for breakfast?"

"Breakfast?" Is he seriously going to fix me breakfast? Usually, he runs away as fast as possible after we've spent the night together.

Ugh. Stop it, Hazel. I agreed to give him a second chance. I can't give him a second chance while holding a grudge about the past.

"I don't have much in my pantry. I was supposed to go grocery shopping yesterday but somehow I didn't get around to it."

He waggles his eyebrows before pulling on his jeans. "Worth it. I'll find something for us to eat, or I'll treat you to a pastry at *Pirate's Pastries.*"

"Oh, what kind of pastry? I could go for a pirate's plunder muffin. Or maybe a shipwreck cookie. Or a Kelpie crunch or Selkie bite."

My stomach rumbles in agreement. Parker makes the best pastries. She should be working in some famous patisserie in New York City or Paris. But I'm glad she's not. Especially since she fell in love with a billionaire and now he's moving his entire business to the island.

Miles chuckles. "You better get dressed if you want to go to *Pirate's Pastries.*"

I jump out of bed and rush toward the attached bathroom. "I won't be ten minutes."

He barks out a laugh. "You need more than ten minutes to dry your hair."

I rush through my morning routine, although I don't bother drying my hair. It'll be a mess of curls I can't get a brush through later but I don't want Miles to wait any longer. Assuming he didn't flee already.

When I return to the bedroom to get dressed, I notice a steaming cup of coffee on the bedside table. I take a sip and moan. It's prepared the way I prefer it. Lots of sugar and milk. Yum.

I dress in my usual 'uniform' for days I work as a therapist. Roomy clothes I can move in and comfortable shoes.

I rush into the kitchen – half expecting Miles to be gone – but he's sitting at my table drinking a cup of coffee while playing on his phone.

"You're here." The words escape before I can stop them.

Hurt flashes in his deep blue eyes but he blinks and it's gone. Did I imagine it?

"I'm here. Right where I want to be. Although." He waggles his eyebrows. "I wouldn't have minded staying in bed for another round."

I wag my finger at him. "What about the whole 'we won't have sex until you understand I'm serious about you'-thing?"

He stands and prowls toward me. I try to back up but end up hitting the wall. He slams his palms against the wall to cage me in.

"Do you need me to show you how serious I am about you again? Because I can."

My breath hitches. I want him to show me again. And again. My panties dampen and my nipples tighten as memories of how well Miles can show me he's serious flitter through my mind.

He nips my chin. "What time is your first patient?"

I tilt my head to offer him better access. "Nine."

He swears under his breath before stepping away. "It's after eight. I need to get you fed before your first patient arrives."

My mouth gapes open. "You'd rather eat than get naked with me?"

His blue eyes darken until they're practically violet. "Don't get me wrong. I always want to get naked with you. But I need to take care of you, too. And you need to eat before you start work. I don't want you hungry when dealing with patients."

I scowl. How am I supposed to keep my distance from him and keep my heart safe when he's being this sweet?

He drops a feather soft kiss onto my lips and my scowl disappears. "Let's get you fed before you get cranky."

"I don't get cranky when I'm hungry."

He tweaks my nose. "Sure, you don't."

We're holding hands when we enter *Pirate's Pastries* ten minutes later. The line is long with people waiting to get their coffee and muffin fix. But it moves quickly, and soon enough it's our turn.

"Yes!" Parker shouts when she sees us. "I knew you two would work things out."

I narrow my eyes at her. "Knew we'd work things out or bet we would?"

I should have known. Smugglers love betting. Especially when the wager involves locals. Who's getting married and when. Who's pregnant. Will the baby be a boy or girl. The list goes on and on.

Parker shrugs. "Same thing."

"Betting is fueled by gossip. I thought you hated gossip."

"No one's gossiping about you. We're merely interested in how you are doing."

"I prefer the old you before you fell in love with a billionaire."

I'm lying. I didn't enjoy watching Parker struggle one bit. No one understood why the bakery was in trouble. It was always crowded. No one realized Parker was trying to repair her relationship with her parents with money. I will forever be in Jeremy's debt for loving Parker and convincing her that her parents don't deserve her hard-earned money.

Parker's smile stretches from ear to ear. "Jeremy is the best."

I nod to Miles. "This guy isn't too bad either."

Miles throws an arm around my shoulders. "Isn't too bad? Do I need to prove I'm pretty damn good again? You'll be late for your first patient."

I wish I could be late. But people take time out of their work days to visit a physical therapist. It would be unfair of me to be late and have them miss even more work time.

I elbow Miles. "Behave."

Parker giggles. "I'll take words I never expected to hear Hazel Harris speak for five-hundred dollars."

I frown. "I behave."

She snorts. "Sure, you do. And you've never tried to steal Viking before either."

"I thought I found a loophole."

Every summer, the residents of the island try to steal the live mascots. I decided to steal Viking – he's the most tame and easiest to handle of the mascots – but I was told in no uncertain terminology by the mayor, I couldn't steal the otter since I'm a resident of Smuggler's Rest, which is the town Viking is the mascot for.

I peer around the counter. "Where is Smuggler's Rest most famous resident, anyway? I want my otter cuddles."

"He's sleeping beneath the ovens."

"I guess I'm visiting the kitchen." I start to go around the counter but Miles shackles my wrist to stop me.

"You need to eat your muffin and drink your coffee. You have less than fifteen minutes before your first patient arrives."

Parker gasps. "Does Miles sound concerned about you being on time, or am I having hallucinations?"

I giggle. "I've thought I was having hallucinations plenty of times recently."

She groans. "Don't tell me you're harvesting mushrooms again."

"I never harvested mushrooms. It was one mushroom."

Miles grunts. "And it was a mistake."

I wag a finger at him. "Don't be annoyed because I thought you were a purple elephant."

"You screamed I was going to crush you."

"I don't remember. Therefore, it's not true."

He rolls his eyes. "Likely excuse."

Parker hands him two coffees and a bag. "Here's your order. Go sit down and eat before the people in the line riot for having to wait too long."

"I'm not going to riot," Sloane says from behind us. "I am going to change my bet about when these two lovebirds finally make things official, though."

I groan. How did I not notice her standing behind us in line? I blame Miles. I forget to monitor my surroundings when he's around.

"Behave," he mutters to Sloane before leading me to a table in the corner. "Ignore them. They don't matter. The only people who matter in this relationship are me and you."

"Pretty words, surfer boy."

He hands me my coffee and muffin. "I'll say all the pretty words in the world until you're convinced I'm serious."

"And then you'll let yourself go? Grunt all the time. Wear sweatpants and gain weight from all the beer you drink."

"Don't worry, Blaze. I plan to spoil you every single day for the rest of our lives."

I want to tell him I love him. I want him to spoil me every single day. I want to be with him for the rest of our lives.

But I've been burned once by Miles. And I barely survived. I don't know if I can handle it a second time.

Chapter 28

I expect Kai and Zane to surprise me. Not Eli.

Miles

I whistle as I stroll into *Buccaneer's Distillery*. Monday mornings usually suck but any morning I wake up wrapped around Hazel is a good morning. And making out with her at her practice before I hopped in my car to come here didn't hurt either.

"Good morning, Miles," Dakota greets from the reception area. She's technically Eli's assistant, but she's also the unofficial receptionist for the distillery.

"Good morn—"

Kai and Zane rush into the area.

"Good. You're here."

I frown at Zane. "Of course, I'm here. This is where I work."

Kai snorts. "Where you work when you aren't surfing."

I scowl. He makes it sound as if I'm never in the office. Trust me. I'm in this office way more than I want to be. Sitting behind a desk all day is not my definition of fun.

"At least I'm not a goofball who made Jaxon do my work for me."

"Made. Past tense. I'm not a goofball anymore."

Zane barks out a laugh. "And you didn't spend an hour speaking with a German accent to a newspaper reporter."

"In my defense, he thought I was German. I just rolled with it."

"Until the reporter asked if it would be easier to conduct the interview in German. Then, you panicked."

Kai frowns. "I didn't panic."

"You ran out of the room screaming 'I have ze diarrhea'."

Kai shrugs. "Maybe it was true."

"This has been fun. But I need to prepare for my meeting with Eli." I try walking around my brothers to my office but Zane stops me.

"I need you to sign off on this marketing plan."

"I don't—"

He slaps a pen in my hand. "Sign it."

I glance down at the clipboard. There's nothing to sign. It's a blank piece of paper. "Why are you…" I trail off when I realize my hand is now covered in blue ink.

"Exploding pen prank." I roll my eyes. "Not very original."

I hand him the pen and clipboard before making my way to the restrooms. I rinse my hands under the water before pumping soap onto them. I lather my hands up and scrub them but when I go to dry my hands, I notice they're now bright red.

What the hell?

I wash my hands again but it doesn't do much to diminish the red coloring. In fact, my hands now have a distinctive rainbow color.

I march out of the restroom intent on finding my brothers to give them a piece of my mind. I don't have to go far. They're waiting in the hallway for me.

"Ha!" Zane points at my hands. "It's a rainbow of flavor."

Kai claps. "This worked out better than I expected."

"You're both assholes."

"Assholes who should be working," Rhett hollers from his office.

"Spoil sport." Kai sticks his tongue out at Rhett's office.

"I saw that!"

"You didn't see anything. Because I didn't do anything." Kai hurries toward the distillery area. "I need to go check on a … something. There's something I should be checking on."

Rhett stands in his doorway and watches Kai scurry away. "You two get back to work."

I hold up my hands. "This isn't my fault."

Zane chuckles. "You shouldn't have bragged about winning the prank war."

"It's not bragging if it's true."

And it is true. My brothers are too busy falling in love and having offspring to worry about the prank war. I can multitask. I can convince Hazel to give me a second chance while winning the prank war against my brothers.

"Whatever," he mutters before stomping toward the nursery. "I'm going to visit Adele."

I still can't believe there's an actual nursery in the distillery offices. Two years ago, I would have thought the nursery was a prank. Now all my brothers are paired off and either have children or want to.

I used to think my brothers were lame but when I found out Hazel might leave the island, I realized I was the lame one. Pushing her away because I was miserable. Because I thought I wasn't worthy of love after I screwed up the career I'd always dreamed of.

Dakota strolls into the hallway and Rhett lights up. "Hey, Havoc."

She settles herself against Rhett before telling me, "Eli's ready for you."

"But I haven't had time to prepare."

She shrugs. "It's not my fault you were playing with your brothers and lost track of time."

"I wasn't playing."

She nods to my hands. "Agree to disagree."

I scowl. This isn't a joke. I'm meeting with Eli today to discuss the approach to our meeting with *Velvet Blossom.* I want to prove to my big brother that I'm ready to meet with the distillery's biggest clients.

I glance down at my rainbow hands. I'm not proving anything to him today except for my lack of seriousness.

"How do I get rid of dye on my hands?"

"In the next thirty seconds?" Dakota snorts. "You don't."

"When did you become cruel?"

She blinks. "I'm the cruel one? You're the one who bought our five-year-old a drum set for Christmas."

"Pearl loves her drum set. I think she has real talent."

"Said by the man who doesn't have to listen to her practice at all hours of the day and night," Rhett grumbles.

I shrug. "Practice is important for every musician."

"She's five."

"Taylor Swift was sixteen when she had her first hit."

Dakota buries her face in Rhett's shoulder. "And now we know why she keeps saying she's going to be the next Taylor Swift."

"I'm confused. You don't want your daughter to be a talented musician?"

Rhett grunts. "She wrote a song about how worms eat poop yesterday."

"It's better than writing a song about getting her heart broken."

Rhett groans. "My daughter is forbidden from dating until she's twenty-five."

Dakota tugs on his shirt. "I think you mean our daughter can date when she's a teenager."

"And in the meantime, she can practice her drums."

Rhett lunges for me but I dodge him and dart into Eli's office.

Eli's brow wrinkles. "Why are you out of breath?"

"Long story."

"Do I even want to know why your hands are rainbow-colored?"

"Because my brothers are assholes."

He lifts a brow.

"Two of my brothers are assholes."

He scowls. "I thought you were taking your work more seriously. It's the reason I agreed to let you come with me to the meeting with *Velvet Blossom*."

"I should be at the meeting regardless. I am the sales manager for the distillery, and the restaurant chain is one of our biggest customers."

He grins. "Right answer."

I scowl. "You were tricking me?"

"You can't blame me. I started *Buccaneer's* with this grand idea of all of my brothers working together on Smuggler's Hideaway. But you, Kai, and Zane treated the distillery like a joke."

"No, we didn't."

"Kai let Jaxon handle his responsibilities as operations manager. Zane jetted off to the other side of the world every chance he got. And you spent more time surfing than in the office."

"It's hard to give up on a dream."

He slaps my shoulder. "I understand, which is why I never pushed any of you. You were all much younger, and this distillery wasn't your dream."

"Yeah, well, I can't have my dream job."

No matter how many years have passed since my accident in Hawaii, my stomach still sours at having to give up my dream of becoming a pro surfer. I was good. Really good.

I could have won the world championships. Gotten sponsorships from all the big brands. Traveled the world for competitions. Instead, I'm here. Stuck behind a desk selling whiskey and moonshine.

"I'm sorry, Miles. If I could change things, I would. Hell, I even asked Jeremy to design a new shoulder for you."

"You did?"

"Damn straight. Do you think I enjoy watching my brother's dreams get destroyed?" He shakes his head. "When I arrived at the hospital in Hawaii… The doctors weren't sure of the damage. They were worried about your head injury. About how long you'd been underwater. I was fucking terrified. And lying to Mom that your injury wasn't serious."

I remember Eli being there when I woke up in the hospital – disoriented and in pain. But he never seemed worried. He was my cool, calm, competent older brother.

"Rhett and I discussed not offering you a job at the distillery. We both wanted you to find your own path. But when you returned home, all lost, I couldn't not offer you a job."

"And now I'm stuck behind a desk for the rest of my life."

He wags his finger. "Not if you impress me at the meeting with *Velvet Blossom.* This is your opportunity to show me you can handle the big clients and our distributors."

I blow out a breath. He's right. I was too busy whining and complaining about life to realize this job doesn't have to be a desk job every day. There are chances for me to get out and see the world. Not on a surfboard, but a surfboard isn't everything. Some people are more important than chasing the waves.

"Okay. Let's discuss strategy."

Chapter 29

Exercise bands should be classified as weapons.

HAZEL

"Come on," I push. "You can do one more rep."

"You're cruel. This is cruel and unusual punishment," Addy whines.

"Punishment is not being able to use your arm correctly for the rest of your life. Do your exercises, or you won't be able to hold the microphone while you're singing for more than one song. You'll be one of those singers who uses a headset. Lame."

Addy currently works as a waitress at *Five Fathoms Brewing*, but her true love is singing. She plays piano and writes her own songs. She's amazing. But if she wants to earn her living through music, she'll need to take a risk and leave this island.

"I changed my mind. You're not cruel. You're mean."

"And right."

"Whatever." She huffs before pulling on the resistance band until it's taut.

"Good. Now slowly release."

The band snaps out of her hands and flies forward. I duck before it hits me in the face. It lands on the mirror with a splat before falling to the ground.

"Oops. Sorry." Judging by the twinkle in her eyes, she's not sorry at all. Maybe sorry she missed my face.

"At least I'm only mean with words. I don't actually try to hit people."

"No?" She waggles her eyebrows. "You don't ever hit Miles when he annoys you?"

I sigh. Patient after patient this morning has tried to gather information about my relationship with Miles. The wager on the bet must be sky-high. No one's ever been this curious about my love life before.

I check my watch. "We have a few more minutes. Let's work on some core exercises."

She groans. "Not the exercise ball again."

I roll the ball her way. "Your throne, milady."

"Stupid exercise ball," she mutters before flouncing down on it.

Expert tip: Never flounce down on an exercise ball. The ball bounces and Addy jumps to her feet. The ball rolls toward her and she kicks out, causing the ball to fly forward straight into my stomach.

"Oof!" I bend over to wrap my arms around my stomach.

"Oopsie!"

"You could at least pretend to be sorry."

"Even when I'm not?"

I glare at her. "I'm booing you off the stage the next time you sing karaoke."

"You can try. Your boos won't be heard over the cheers."

I fist my hands at my hips. "Did you forget about my megaphone?"

She groans. "How could I forget? You used it to wake up my entire neighborhood back in high school."

"I was only trying to wake up Sandra. How dare she say she kissed Miles!"

I knew Sandra was lying, but she needed to learn her lesson. Liars do not get to sleep through the night on the night before senior pictures are taken. Guess whose picture is not in the yearbook.

Addy rubs her hands together. "And we're back to Miles."

"I'll talk about Miles." She smiles. "If you do ten more reps with the resistance band."

"Nope." She shakes her head. "No pot of gold is worth another ten reps."

"Wimp."

"Torturer."

The bell over the front door rings as my next patient enters the practice. Addy doesn't hesitate. She grabs her purse and rushes to the exit. "See you next week!"

I follow her to the front door. "You must be my mystery patient," I greet Hudson.

He smiles. "Sorry. I asked my secretary to be discreet."

I frown. "Discreet? Are you having issues from your football injury and keeping it from Nova?"

"Have you ever tried to keep a secret from Nova?" He chuckles. "Impossible."

True. Nova is one of the biggest troublemakers on the island. Which is saying a lot considering the island is full of troublemakers. How the Raider brothers haven't blown up the island by now is beyond me.

"Why the discreet appointment, then?"

"I wanted to discuss the job offer."

"I—"

He holds up a hand to cut me off. "Before you say anything, please know I am serious about offering you this job. This has nothing to do with Miles."

Good. Because, as we've established, Miles does not and will not control me.

"I'm listening."

"What I'm about to tell you is a secret. I trust you to not tell anyone."

"My curiosity is officially piqued."

"My old NFL team is staying at the resort for training camp this summer. Training camp is happening at a nearby college on the mainland but no other accommodations could guarantee the players' privacy. I can."

The Hideaway Haven Resort was designed to give celebrities privacy. Probably because Hudson was living as a hermit when the resort was built. The security is tight. Not even the worst troublemakers attempt to pull pranks there.

"You think this information is secret?"

He drops his chin to his chest and swears under his breath. "Does everyone know?"

My nose wrinkles. "Pretty much."

"If the press catches wind of the team staying, the resort will lose credibility. We have a reputation for providing privacy for our guests."

I scowl. "You can't seriously believe anyone on the island would contact the press?"

He sighs. "I don't worry about smugglers. I worry about the tourists."

I flick my hand in dismissal. "Smugglers don't discuss Hideaway business when tourists are present."

He rubs a hand over his jaw. "Why do I have the feeling this training camp is going to be the death of me?"

"Don't exaggerate. It'll be fun. Can you imagine a bunch of extra-large football players doing mermaid karaoke?"

He groans. "They'll be riots."

I waggle my eyebrows. "But it'll be fun."

He shakes his head. "No wonder you and Miles are the perfect couple. You're both perfectly insane."

"Ah, thanks."

"Moving on. As part of the agreement with the team, I promised to have a physical therapist on site at the resort."

I lift an eyebrow. "And who, pray mermaids tell, is your physical therapist?"

"I'm hoping you."

I purse my lips. "I have other offers."

"I heard." He pulls an envelope out of his pocket. "Which is why I increased my initial offer."

"What initial offer?" I mutter as I remove the letter. As I scan it, my eyes widen further and further. He can't be serious. "This is ridiculous."

The offer from the VA hospital can't compare to this. The income is better, the number of vacation days is higher. There's even a generous retirement plan.

"My goal is to have the NFL team return every summer for training camp. I need a physical therapist who can be on hand every summer to support the players."

"There's no reason to hire me full-time. We can do a temporary contract for five weeks in the summer. Or you can find another therapist to temporarily work for you."

"I don't want someone to come and go. I want someone who's on hand all year long. If a guest is injured learning how to surf or jumping off a boat, I want a therapist on hand to help them until they can get home."

I wave the letter at him. "And you're willing to pay."

He snorts. "You have no idea how much the NFL pays. If you were a therapist for a team, you'd earn double my offer."

"Hmm… maybe you can hook me up with the manager of your old team."

"And have to sleep with one eye open for the rest of my life while I wait for Miles to exact his revenge? No thanks. I have a family."

"Miles doesn't control me."

"He'll still lose his mind when he realizes you're in the locker room with forty-eight naked players."

"Naked? Do they run around the locker room naked? Do they have towel fights?"

Hudson chuckles. "Everyone on this island is crazy."

"Hey! You grew up here, too."

He nods to the letter. "What do you say? The terms are negotiable."

I raise my eyebrows. "You'd pay me more than this?"

"If necessary."

"I don't know if you're insane or have too much money you don't know what to do with."

"No one has too much money when you have children to put through college."

"Children?" Hudson and Nova only have one child – Iliana.

"Nova wants more. But she's not pregnant. If I hear a rumor she's pregnant, I'm rescinding this offer."

I hold up my hands. "I do not spread rumors."

"Liar."

"Correction. I don't start rumors."

He chuckles. "All smugglers are troublemakers."

"But you want to hire me anyway."

"I do. Take some time to review the offer. I'll be waiting for your response."

I wait until he's gone before I sink into a chair. Holy mermaids in smuggler's water! This offer makes it possible for me to stay on the island. Doing what I love.

The only compromise is I'd have an employer. I'd no longer have control over my time schedule. I'd be on call seven days a week.

Not a big compromise to stay on the island where the man I love lives.

Nope. I'm not doing this. I'm not making life decisions based on Miles. Not when there's a chance he dumps me again.

Chapter 30

In case anyone's confused, I've never had a poison ivy rash on my ass.

Miles

The door to the apartment building flies open and Hazel rushes out. "Sorry, I'm late."

I capture her wrist before she runs down the sidewalk. "Hold on. You didn't say hi."

"Hi, surfer boy. Now, come on. We can't be late. I want a good seat."

I palm her neck and draw her near. "This is how you say hello to me."

I meld my lips to hers. She sighs and I thrust my tongue into her mouth. Her taste hits me and I groan. I could live on her taste alone. I don't need anything else.

Honk! Honk!

I startle when the car blares its horn and tear my lips from Hazel's. I glare at the car. My brother, Rhett, waves. I give him the finger.

I thread my fingers through Hazel's and lead her toward the sidewalk. "My brothers are assholes."

"You won't hear me argue with you. Remember the time Kai doused your bed with water?"

I groan. "He thought it'd seem as if I wet the bed when I brought you home."

"No one has that much urine in their bladder." She giggles and her nose scrunches. I can't resist kissing it. She pushes me away. "Knock it off. I don't want to be late."

"Do you have a story to tell?"

Tonight is the *Foam & Fable Storytelling Night* at the *Five Fathoms Brewing* restaurant. Everyone is encouraged to take the mic and tell a story. Once the story is finished, the crowd votes on whether the tale is true or bogus. Or they can merely tell you to 'walk the plank', which is a punishment to drink a pint. At the end of the evening, the crowd votes on who told the best story. The winner doesn't have to pay for their meal or drinks.
"I'm not telling." Hazel mimics zipping her lips.

"You're afraid I'll figure out if it's true or bogus."

"You're cute. As if you can tell when I'm lying."

"Trust me. I can tell when you're lying."

She scowls. "If you mention the wrinkle on my forehead again, I'm going to headbutt you."

I chuckle. "Headbutt me? Someone's feeling violent tonight."

"I want to win."

"Little Miss Competitive strikes again."

"You're one to talk," she mutters but she doesn't deny her competitive nature. She can't. I know her too well for her to lie to me and she knows it.

We round the corner and reach the parking lot of *Five Fathoms Brewing.* The bar and restaurant is in a restored barn, whereas the brewing facilities are across the parking lot.

"Is it my imagination, or did they double the size of their brewing facilities after the hurricane?"

I snort. "If Eli had his way, the size would have quadrupled."

"I still can't believe your big brother insisted Paisley brew beer at the distillery. Those two hated each other."

"And yet they're now living together and have a baby."

It gives me hope. If Paisley could forgive Eli for being a jerk in high school, maybe Hazel can forgive me for how I treated her.

"Speaking of Eli." Hazel points to my big brother and his fiancée.

I groan. "I was hoping to have a night without my family."

"Why?" She narrows her eyes at me. "Are you embarrassed of me?"

I throw an arm over her shoulders. "More worried about how much they're going to embarrass me."

She rubs her hands together. "This sounds promising. Do you think he'll tell embarrassing baby stories about you?"

"No one can stop us!" Rhett shouts as he escorts Dakota into the restaurant.

"I was already looking forward to tonight, but this is going to be even better than I expected."

Hazel gazes up at me with a smile on her pretty pink lips and a twinkle in her green eyes. Happiness practically radiates from her. If my being embarrassed by my brothers makes her this happy, my brothers can have at it.

I'll do anything to make my woman happy. She deserves all the happiness in the world after how I've treated her over the past years. But those days are over.

Addy groans when we enter the restaurant. "Are all of the Raider brothers coming tonight?"

I shrug. "No idea."

She surveys the map of tables. "Okay. I'll separate you. No Raider next to another Raider."

Hazel laughs. "Because separating the brothers worked so well at school."

"I'm doing the best I can here." Addy grabs two menus and leads us to our table right in front of the stage.

Once we're alone, Hazel leans across the table. "How much cash did you slip her to get us the best seat in the house?"

"None."

She raises an eyebrow and I can't lie to her. I want her to know I'll always tell her the truth. No matter how bad it makes me look.

"I promised her a discount on her next purchase from the distillery."

"Good thing you're the sales manager."

I open my mouth to make a derogatory comment about my job but close it again when I realize my job isn't as bad as I thought it was. Especially since I've got several trips lined up. Huh. Never thought I'd appreciate my job.

Chloe, the manager of the restaurant, jumps on the stage. "Good evening, smugglers and mermaids!" The crowd erupts in cheers. She waits until everyone settles down. "Are you ready for the *Foam & Fable Storytelling Night?*"

The crowd goes completely nuts – stomping their feet, whistling, clapping, and shouting. Typical smuggler behavior.

"Our first storytelling smuggler is the one, the only, Eli Raider!"

Eli swaggers past our table. He winks at me. Shit. He's definitely telling an embarrassing story about me. Good thing Hazel knows most of my embarrassing past. Because she was right there beside me.

Hazel reaches across the table and grasps my hand. "Don't worry. I'll stand by your side."

My chest warms. This is what I want. I want Hazel to stand by my side forever. Through marriage and children and career changes. Through all the hard shit life will throw at us.

I lean over the table to kiss her. "Thank you," I murmur against her lips.

"You're my surfer boy. No thanks needed."

Eli clears his throat. "This is a story about my brother, Miles." I groan. I knew it. "All six of us Raider brothers went camping for the weekend. Zane wanted to become a Boy Scout but Rhett said he could only join if he agreed to go camping for a weekend. And off the Raider brothers went for a weekend of camping.

Unfortunately, none of us had camped before, so we weren't exactly prepared. We forgot all kinds of things – fuel for the camping fire, extra batteries for the flashlights. But, worst of all, we forgot toilet paper. No teenage boy who's been gorging himself on hot dogs and s'mores all day can avoid nature's call. Off Miles went to 'use the facilities'. No one thought anything of it, until a telltale rash appeared a week later. Poison ivy!"

"Bogus!" I shout. "Kai got poison ivy on his ass, not me."

"Bogus! Bogus! Bogus!" The crowd chants.

"Walk the plank!" Hazel shouts.

Addy arrives with a shot of moonshine and a beer. She hands them to Eli, who frowns before drinking both. He jumps from the stage and walks to his table, where Paisley is laughing at him.

Chloe steps back on stage. "Our next storyteller is Hazel Harris. It's gonna be outrageous. I'm betting it's bogus. Here comes Hazel!"

Hazel stands and I squeeze her hand. "Go show them how it's done."

"I will." She winks before moving to the stage and grabbing the mic.

"Here is the tale of the moonshine watermelon bomb." She narrows her eyes at the crowd. "It's so unbelievable, it's true."

"Bogus!" Kai shouts. I search the crowd until I find him. He waves and I scratch my forehead with my middle finger.

"Like all great tales, this one started innocent enough. I wanted to make a watermelon soaked in moonshine for the

Fourth of July. Except the fourth arrived and I forgot all about my poor, innocent watermelon.

Until the next weekend, when I needed a dish to bring to Sunday dinner with the family. I barely had a chance to set the watermelon on the table before Thomas arrived with a big knife to slice it open. He barely touched the watermelon before the thing exploded like it was harboring bootleg fireworks. Seeds flew everywhere. The grill was covered in watermelon guts. Everyone screamed.

And I swear to Poseidon, a seagull took a direct hit and came back for vengeance. The next thing we know, we're under aerial assault. Seagulls diving for us, pooping everywhere. It was a massacre. Sticky. Terrifying. Beautiful."

"Bogus!" Zane shouts.

Hazel lifts her eyebrow. "If the crowd claims my story is bogus, but it's true, I automatically win."

"She's bluffing!" Rhett shouts.

The crowd takes up a chant. "Bogus! Bogus! Bogus!"

Hazel smirks as she pulls out her phone. "Good thing I have proof."

Chloe rushes to help her attach her phone to the beamer, and soon enough, a video of seagulls attacking a picnic is showing. Thomas stands in the middle of the chaos, covered in watermelon as seagulls divebomb him.

Chloe grabs Hazel's wrist and raises her arm in the air. "We have a winner!"

Hazel bows before returning to our table, where I sweep her into my arms and meld my lips to hers. "Congrats, Blaze."

"Do not shove your hard dick into me. We're staying. We eat and drink for free all night."

My cock whimpers but I bark out a laugh. This is my woman. Crazy. Impulsive. Fun as hell. And sexy as can be. I don't mind spending the entire night watching her brag about her win to the other Smugglers. I'll probably end up in a fist fight.

Worth it. She's worth everything.

Chapter 31

I'll take mythical creatures for five-hundred.

Hazel

"Hey, Parker," I greet the bakery owner as I step inside *Pirate's Pastries.* "How are you doing?"

Her nostrils flare. "I'm as mad as a kraken and ready to rain down vengeance like a leviathan."

I bite my tongue to stop from laughing at her references to mythical sea creatures. I don't want her going all leviathan on me. Being on the receiving end of vengeance is never fun. Doling it out, on the other hand? Oodles of joy.

"What happened?"

"Jeremy put a swimming pool in our backyard."

"How dare he? This is outrageous. A billionaire put a swimming pool in his backyard. What was he thinking? Maybe we should contact the police."

She crosses her arms over her chest and glares at me. "He shouldn't be spending all his money on our house. We don't need a pool. Or a chef's kitchen. Or fifty bathrooms."

I lift my eyebrow. "Fifty bathrooms?"

"Slight exaggeration for dramatic purposes."

I nod. "I'll allow it."

"He shouldn't be spending his money on me."

I scowl. "Why not?"

"It's ridiculous. I don't need it."

"Parker, he loves you and wants to spoil you."

She blows out a breath, and her shoulders sag as the tension flows out of her body. "I know but how am I supposed to spoil him?"

"I have a few ideas."

She glares at me. "If you mention sexual favors, I'm kicking you out of here and banning you for life."

I wag my finger at her. "Ban me for life and I'll be forced to steal Viking."

"Good luck. Mr. Moneybags bought him a new cage, bed, and security."

"Viking has his own security? What is it? Tough otter bodyguards who hiss and glare at you when you come too close to Viking?"

"Wouldn't you like to know."

Actually, I would. It's important to know how to steal a live mascot. Even if the live mascot is from your town and you're 'not supposed' to steal him. But there's no way Parker will tell me what security measures she's added. She loves Viking too much to allow him to be stolen by the residents.

"There's no reason to ban me. I wasn't actually referring to sexual favors. There are other ways to spoil your billionaire lover. You can bring home coffee and treats. Show up at his office with lunch because he's too busy to take a break. Get pregnant because he's dying to give you children."

"You had me until the end."

I shrug. "I couldn't help myself."

"You never can," she mutters. "What can I get you?"

"Two humongous coffees and whatever treats you have left since it's the end of the day."

She waggles her eyebrows. "Going to see Miles?"

"We're meeting at his surf shack."

"The love shack!"

"At least you're not as mad as a kraken anymore."

She laughs as she hands me my order. "I can never stay mad at Jeremy for long. Which he knows and uses to his advantage."

I smile at her grumbling. "Have a good night."

I sip on my coffee as I walk to the beach. It's not far. Nothing is in Smuggler's Hideaway.

I reach the sand and kick off my shoes before gathering them in my hand and continuing my journey to the surf shack. Love shack isn't too far from the truth either. The number of times Miles and I made out in the shack as teenagers.

I frown when I reach the surf shack. There's a for sale sign on the building.

"What's going on?"

Miles motions to the sign. "Isn't it obvious?"

"Um, no. Because the Miles Raider I know would never give up on his surf shack."

He kisses me quick before snagging a coffee. "Maybe I'm not the Miles Raider you knew anymore."

I scowl. He's the Miles Raider I've known and loved for years. I open my mouth and nearly tell him as much but stop before the words can escape.

I'm not ready to admit I love him. Not out loud at least. I need to be a bit more secure in our relationship and his commitment to me before I admit how I feel.

And when will that be?

I don't know. I honestly don't know how Miles can prove to me he's serious about me and staying on Smuggler's Hideaway.

"Not the Miles I know? Has your body been overtaken by aliens? I thought aliens just probed you and let you go."

"I've never been probed by an alien."

I raise my eyebrows. "You didn't claim to be probed by an alien as an excuse for not finishing your English homework junior year?"

"Can you blame me? We were supposed to read *The Catcher in the Rye.* Holden's voice was so whiny it was cringeworthy."

"I liked the book."

He snorts. "You didn't like the book. You liked how Scarlett made extensive notes about the book when she was a junior. You never even read it."

I gasp. "I did, too."

He cocks an eyebrow.

"Fine. I read the first two chapters. Holden is completely unrelatable. Why are we still reading this book in the twenty-first century?"

Miles smiles and those blue eyes I love to stare into when he's moving deep inside me twinkle. My breath gets caught in my throat. I want those eyes to twinkle at me every day for the rest of my life.

I force those thoughts away. I can't stand here and contemplate my future with Miles when he's right in front of me. Especially since he claims he can read my mind.

I motion to the shack. "What's the deal?"

He shrugs. "I don't need it anymore."

"Miles."

"What? I don't."

"But you love to surf. And you love to give lessons."

"Actually, I could do without the lessons." He rubs his injured shoulder.

"I'm sorry. It sucks you got hurt saving a student."

"Nothing to be sorry about. Besides, it gave me an excuse to spend time with my favorite physical therapist on the island." He winks.

"I'm the only physical therapist on the island."

"You're still my favorite."

"Thank you. Most of my clients have secret fantasies about trapping me under the motor of a treadmill."

"Nah. Those fantasies aren't secret. They write about them in their reviews."

"Gee. Thanks. Way to make me feel loved."

He stalks toward me. I have to lock my limbs in order to hold my ground. He tucks a curl behind my ear. "I can show you how much I love you."

I nod to the shack. "You used to show me in your shack, but now you're selling it."

"It's not sold yet. We could go for one last hurrah?"

I shove him away and he stumbles in the sand. "One last hurrah?"

He chuckles. "For old times' sake."

"Miles Raider, behave!"

"Why start now?"

I shake my head, but I can't help a smile from forming. Miles has and always will test my patience. He pushes all my buttons. And not just the sexy buttons. The 'how far can I push her until she breaks' button gets used an awful lot, too.

"I'm serious, surfer boy. Why are you selling your shack?"

"I don't have time to give lessons anymore. The distillery is getting busier, and I've taken on a more active role as sales manager."

I wait for him to make a derogatory comment about his job but he doesn't. He actually appears happy. He's growing up. Accepting his future won't include being a surfer on the pro circuit. Maybe this time our relationship will last.

"Stopping with lessons doesn't mean you need to sell the shack."

"I don't need all the storage for the equipment for lessons anymore."

"But what about the shower for after you're done surfing? Or the refrigerator the entire Raider clan uses during summer days at the beach?"

"The Raider clan can learn to drag a wagon filled with supplies onto the beach the way the other locals do."

"But you use the refrigerator, too. Are you going to drag a wagon onto the beach?"

"Once we have kids and need a gazillion supplies."

My mouth drops open. Is he seriously discussing us having kids? We have never discussed having kids.

Don't get me wrong. Miles has made it clear he wants children. And I've told him I want children as well. But we've never talked about *us* having kids.

"Why do tiny creatures need so many supplies anyway? It makes no sense," he continues as if he didn't just rock my world.

"You're serious?"

"I've made myself perfectly clear, Blaze. I love you, and I'm not going anywhere. You want children. I want children. Makes sense, we have children together since we will be together."

My heart batters against my chest. For a second, I forget how to breathe. Miles is discussing us having children as if it's a foregone conclusion. Miles. The man who's been hot and cold to me for years.

I can't. I can't think about this right now. I'll end up hyperventilating if I do. Passing out in the sand is no fun.

I motion to the shack. "I meant, are you serious about selling?"

He palms my neck and leans his forehead against mine. "I don't need the surf shack anymore. All I need is us."

Hope blossoms in my stomach and spreads throughout my body. This might work. This time, Miles and I might make it the distance.

I push up on my tiptoes and press my lips to his.

Chapter 32

That wasn't the ending I planned.

Miles

The second Hazel's lips touch mine, I'm lost. Lost in the memories of how often we made out right here on this beach near my shack as teenagers. Lost in the taste of her. Lost in thoughts of our future.

She sighs and I sink my tongue into her mouth. Her fingernails dig into my shoulders and I draw her near until her breasts are pushed up against my chest. It's not enough. I want her naked and writhing against me.

I wrench my mouth from hers. Her lips are swollen from our kisses and I nearly forget why I stopped kissing her.

The waves crash against the shore and I remember. We're in public.

"We should go somewhere private."

She waggles her eyebrows. "Or risk being arrested for indecent behavior?"

"As much as I enjoy getting arrested with you, you're mine to protect. And I wouldn't be doing a good job protecting you if I allowed every man on Smuggler's Hideaway to see you naked."

"Every man? Are we going to parade around the island naked?"

"Smart ass. You know what I meant."

"My ass is very smart, thank you." She wiggles her ass and my cock stands up to applaud. It's a huge fan of her ass. It loves watching it jiggle as I sink into her from behind.

"Why don't I lock up the shack and we can go back to my house? Where I can take my time tasting every inch of you."

Her eyes flare. "Good idea but..."

"But what?" I press my hard cock into her stomach. "Worried I can't fulfil all of your wishes?"

I can fulfill all of her wishes and then some. All night long.

She nods to the shack. "One more time for old times' sake?"

"Not worried about getting sand in places it should never be?" I won't let her get sand anywhere inappropriate, but it's always fun to tease her.

She grasps my hand and leads me to the shack. "We'll figure something out."

I shut and lock the door behind us.

"Wow." She scans the area. "It looks so big without all of the surfing equipment. Where is all the surfing equipment anyway?"

"I sold it to Hudson."

Her mouth drops open. "You sold it?"

I tweak her nose. "Don't worry." I motion to the corner. "I still have my boards."

"Boards. Plural. Because one surfboard will never be enough."

"I'm glad you understand."

She twirls around. "You could make this into a beach retreat. You practically have a kitchen already. All you need is a bed and a sofa."

I stalk toward her until we're close enough to touch. "And what would I do with a beach retreat?"

She bites her bottom lip. "I can think of at least one thing."

I nudge her bottom lip free from her teeth. "Only one thing?"

She shrugs. "One thing that has several different acts."

"Several different acts? Do you mean this?" I glide my thumb over her nipple. It hardens and she gasps.

"Yes. Definitely yes."

"Hmm… I think this experiment is better conducted without clothes." I grasp the hem of her t-shirt. "Arms up."

"Nope."

I lift a brow. "Nope?"

She waves a hand over my body. "I want something pretty to look at."

I growl. "I'm a man. I'm not pretty."

She giggles. "Is handsome better?"

"I prefer sexy."

"Fine." She sighs. "Sexy."

I retreat a step. "Your wish is my command."

I whip off my t-shirt and throw it on the ground before pushing my jeans down my legs with my boxers. My cock juts out – hard and ready – aiming for Hazel – the object of its desire.

"Satisfied?" I ask once I'm completely naked.

Her nose wrinkles. "I was hoping for a show."

"Don't you worry. I'll give you a show." I stalk toward her. Her eyes widen as she rakes her gaze over my naked body. She licks her lips as she stares at my cock.

"Keep it up and this won't last long."

She flutters her eyelashes. "Keep what up?"

"Tease," I mutter before lifting her t-shirt up and over her body, revealing her breasts straining against a white lacy bra. I glide my finger along the edge of the bra. "Pretty."

"Me or my bra?"

"You. No contest," I murmur before tracing the trail of freckles across her chest with my tongue. She clutches my shoulders and yanks me closer. I chuckle against her skin. Hazel has never had a hard time making it clear what she wants. Even when we were young, dumb teenagers, she knew what she wanted.

I unhook her bra and drag it down her shoulders before letting it fall to the ground. "This freckle is my favorite," I say as I kiss a large freckle right above the curve of her breast.

"You're obsessed with my freckles."

I lift my head to meet her gaze. "I'm obsessed with everything about you, Blaze. Your body. Your intelligence. Your inability to ignore a challenge. Your fight to create a career for yourself despite your dad's wishes. You amaze me."

Her face softens. "Thank you. You're pretty amazing yourself."

I smile. It's not 'I love you' but it's something.

"Time to show you how amazing I think you are." I snap the button on her jeans and draw the zipper down. I don't waste any more time. I push her jeans down her legs until she's completely naked before me.

"I have a surprise."

She giggles. "If it's your cock, it's not a surprise. We're well acquainted already."

She reaches for me and squeezes my cock. I moan as I thrust into her hand. It wouldn't take me long to come this way. With Hazel's hand wrapped around me.

"This is not the surprise," I manage to say.

She drops to her knees. "Maybe this is."

She takes me into her mouth and my knees nearly buckle. It's been years since I've been buried inside her hot, wet mouth. I thread my hands through her hair to keep myself grounded.

She continues to squeeze me with her hand while she licks and sucks my cock. I close my eyes as I allow the pleasure to flow through me. Nothing else exists at this moment but me and my Blaze. The whole world could burn down around us and I wouldn't care.

It isn't long before my lower back tingles and my balls tighten. I grit my teeth before I come down her throat. I won't be coming anywhere except in her sweet, tight pussy today.

I tug on her hair. "Enough."

She glances up at me with her mouth stretched around my cock and I nearly forget why I asked her to stop.

"I want to come inside you."

She removes her mouth but continues to pump me with her fist. "My mouth is inside me."

I haul her up by her armpits until she's standing in front of me. "I want to come in your warm, wet pussy while it squeezes me."

She shivers. "Okay."

I lead her to the back of the shack. "This is my surprise."

"Why do you have a cot in here?" Her question screams accusation.

"Hey, Blaze." I brush her hair from her face. "I've never used this cot to seduce a woman before. I sleep on it sometimes so I don't miss the first waves in the morning."

She frowns and the wrinkle on her forehead makes an appearance. She doesn't believe me.

"I love you, Blaze. You're the only woman for me. I wasn't lying when I told you I haven't been with another woman for a year."

She searches my face for signs I'm lying. I widen my eyes and do my best to let the love I feel for her shine through. It must work because she sighs.

"Sorry."

"It's okay."

I hope it's okay at least. I've said I love her multiple times. She hasn't said it back, and she obviously doesn't trust me. Will

I ever be able to convince her to give this second chance a real chance?

I push those thoughts away. I have a warm, naked woman I'm obsessed with standing in front of me. I'm not wasting my chance.

I lay down on the cot and tap my thigh. "Climb on."

She straddles me and the cot creaks in response. "Are you sure this cot is strong enough for the two of us?"

I smirk. "We're about to find out."

"If the cot breaks and I end up with sand in unmentionable places, it'll be a long time before I get naked with you again."

I draw my hands along her sides until I reach the underside of her breasts. "I'm willing to take the chance. Are you?"

She arches her back to push her breasts closer to me. "Yes."

I mold and squeeze her breasts until she's writhing in my lap. "Put me inside you."

She squeezes my cock as she lifts up until her pussy is lined up with my cock. She lowers down and I grit my teeth before I thrust into her. Once she's fully seated, she pauses and I squeeze her hips.

"You gonna move?"

"Like this?" She squeezes her inner muscles.

"You're going to kill me."

"Are you challenging me?"

I dig my fingers into her hips. "I'm challenging you to make us both come."

"I can do that."

She places her hands on my chest and lifts up. She lifts and lowers herself on my cock until she's bouncing on top of me.

I can't handle much more. Her breasts are bouncing in my face. Her pussy is squeezing my cock. Her grunts and groans fill the shack.

I sneak my hand between us until I reach her clit. I rub circles around it the way she likes, and she increases her pace as she pants for breath. I thrust up into her every time she sinks down. The sound of flesh hitting flesh fills the room.

"I'm close. Get there."

"Miles."

"Look me in the eyes when you come all over my cock." Her eyes flicker open. "I love you, Blaze. Come for me."

Her head flies back while her pussy strangles my cock as she climaxes. Fuck. Nothing feels better than this. Nothing. I use my hold on her hips to slam her on my cock as my orgasm approaches.

"Blaze," I groan as it hits.

I continue to glide in and out of her until she collapses on my chest. "That was…"

The joints of the cot creak again but this time it wobbles as well. And then – bam! – we fall to the ground.

Hazel lifts her head. "We broke your cot. Mission accomplished."

I bark out a laugh. Only she could make me laugh while my cock is still buried in her pussy and my back is aching from a sudden fall to the ground.

Chapter 33

I just wanted a cup of coffee.

HAZEL

I stretch as I wake up. Nothing can compare to a few good rounds of sex for a good night's sleep. I reach for Miles but the bed next to me is empty.

My stomach dips but I place a hand on it. No need to freak out. I'm in Miles's house. He wouldn't run away with me still in his bed. He'd kick me out of bed first.

Except…Miles has never kicked me out of his bed. He's been extremely uncomfortable. He's rushed off to shower. He's even faked phone calls to avoid conversation. But he's never kicked me out.

Good reminder. Miles might have avoided me for the most part since returning home from Hawaii, but he hasn't always been a complete jerk.

Which is good. Since I love him. I'd hate to be in love with a complete jerk.

I need to figure out a way to tell him. A hand on my stomach doesn't stand a mermaid's chance on land of helping me from spiraling out now. Tell Miles I love him? What a stupid idea. He's enjoying chasing me. What happens when the chase is over? Will the fun be over, too? Will the excitement have died?

I hate this doubt. I never used to question Miles and his feelings. I knew he loved me. I was secure in our relationship. Until he blew my security to smithereens.

Ugh! I pound a fist on the mattress. I hate being this insecure woman. It's not me. I know what I want and I go get it.

I love Miles. It's a fact. An undeniable fact. And the smugglers know I tried to deny it. For years.

It's time to tell him I love him. And face whatever consequences may come.

I'm a grown woman. I can handle consequences. My heart contracts and I clutch my chest as fear slithers its way into my veins.

I grit my teeth and roll out of bed. I am not letting fear rule me. Not anymore.

I snag Miles's sweatshirt from the floor and put it on. It's long enough to be a skirt on me. I stumble to the kitchen.

Miles smiles at me from his seat at the kitchen table. "Good morning, Blaze."

"You're up early."

He chuckles as he stands and kisses my forehead. "Sit. I'll make you a coffee."

I don't argue. If Miles wants to make me coffee, he can make me coffee.

I stare outside at the view as he prepares my drink. It's an awesome view. The beach is visible beyond the copse of trees. Beyond the beach is the sea.

"I could sit here and stare at the water all day," I murmur as Miles hands me a mug.

He squeezes my shoulder. "Sit for as long as you want. If I had my way, you'd never leave."

Never leave? Does he want me to move in with him? Despite my recent decision to tell him I love him, I hold up a hand. "It's too early for that kind of talk."

You may now refer to me as Hazel, the big fat chicken. Or scaredy-cat. Either way is unfortunately accurate.

"It's a good thing you're not a surfer. You'd miss all the good waves."

I motion to the water. "Go ahead. Knock yourself out. I have no intention of being eaten by a shark at this time of the morning."

"But in the afternoon is okay?"

I glare at him. "You know what I meant."

He drags my chair closer until we're touching and kisses my nose. "You're grumpy this morning."

"I didn't get much sleep. Someone…" I poke his chest, "kept me awake most of the night."

He waggles his eyebrows. "I heard no complaints."

And he won't either. I'll take being tired every morning if I can spend every night with Miles getting sweaty in the sheets.

But being tired is not why I'm grumpy. Nope. My whirling mind is to blame for any grumpiness. I can practically hear the ping pong back and forth in my mind. Tell Miles I love him. No, don't tell him. Yes, tell him. No, don't.

It's enough to give anyone a migraine.

"Listen, I...," I begin but then pause since I have no idea where I'm going with this sentence.

"You what?"

I clear my throat in an attempt to buy some time. Lie, Hazel. Lie your pants off. Shit. I'm not wearing any pants.

"I... um..." Way to sound graceful. "Never mind."

"Nope." Miles pinches my chin. "I want to hear what has your mind spinning out of control this morning."

"My mind isn't spinning out of control."

"And there isn't steam coming out of your ears either."

"Fine. I—"

My phone rings and relief slams into me at the interruption.

I start to stand but Miles pushes me back down. "I've got it."

He swaggers to the kitchen counter, where my phone is plugged in next to his. Huh. I don't remember plugging in my phone. And I certainly didn't bring my charger with me.

"I bought an extra charger for your phone in case you ever needed it," Miles answers my unasked question as he hands me my phone.

"You bought a charger?"

He taps my phone. "Don't you need to answer?"

I glance at the display. Major Phillips is calling. I quickly hit ignore.

Miles frowns at my phone. "Why are you getting calls from a major?"

"He's in charge of the physical therapy unit at the VA hospital."

"Still trying to recruit you after you told him no?"

"I didn't tell him no."

Miles freezes. "What?"

"I haven't turned down his offer yet."

He rears back. "What?"

My brow wrinkles. "Why are you confused?"

"I thought you turned down the offer from the VA hospital."

"Why would you think I turned it down? I haven't made up my mind yet."

He scowls. "You've been lying to me."

"Hold on. I haven't lied to you."

"You led me on. You made me think you were staying." He pushes to his feet and retreats to a corner of the kitchen.

I stand and follow him. "I haven't been lying to you."

He lifts an eyebrow. "You haven't? You refuse to tell me you love me."

My heart pounds in my chest. This is not the way I intended to tell him. During an argument about whether I'm staying on the island.

"I…" I trail off. I don't know what to say.

"This is exactly what I'm talking about. I've told you I love you over and over again, but you won't say the words to me. Even though I know you feel them."

How dare he decide how I feel! I cross my arms over my chest. "You know I feel them?"

He ignores the anger emanating from me. "I know you love me. I know you're worried. I've done everything I can to prove to you I'm here to stay. But you won't believe me."

I want to tell him I believe him, but I'm not there yet. I'm ninety-nine percent sure. But the last one percent is holding on for dear life.

"I promise to support whatever decision you make about your job but you won't even discuss the options with me."

Because I need to figure this out for myself. I don't want my decision to be based on a man. It's bad enough I went to a local college to stay near Miles. Especially when he left my junior year for Hawaii. But not before dumping his boring high school girlfriend.

"This is my decision. It has nothing to do with you."

He growls. "Wrong. Whatever decision you make has everything to do with me. I love you." He pounds his chest. "I want to be wherever you are. Hell, if you want to be the physical therapist for the Antarctica mission, I'll go with you."

"You'd freeze your ass off and complain about it all the time."

He cups my cheek. "But I'd be with you. Being with you is all that matters."

I want to reach for him but I still don't trust him. "Is it? I'm all that matters?"

"Yes, Blaze, you are all that matters."

"And if you suddenly get an offer to coach the US surfing team in California? What then?"

He drops his hand. "Not even a remote possibility."

"Bullshit. You'd flee the island so fast there'd be skid marks on the bridge."

"This is what you think?" Pain flashes in his eyes. Pain I caused.

I ignore his pain and plow on. "You've done it before. You were in such a hurry to get to Hawaii to compete in the pro circuit, you couldn't dump me fast enough."

"Because I was an idiot!"

"How do I know you won't be an idiot again?"

"I'm sorry. I never should have dumped you. I was young and dumb. And I didn't want you to put your life on hold for me."

I pound my chest with my fist. "It was my choice to go to college nearby. My choice to wait for you. But you stole that choice from me."

"And now it's my choice to stick around. To stay on the island."

"I find that hard to believe."

He shakes his head. "I thought you were smarter than this."

He grabs his keys and marches toward the door.

"You're leaving? This is why I can't trust you. You run away whenever things get tough."

He halts with his hands on his hips and his head bent forward. "I don't want to leave, but I'm terrified I'll say something stupid. Something you'll use against me in every argument we have in the future."

I want to tell him he's wrong but I'd be a liar. I'm the queen of holding grudges.

"My phone is on for you night and day if you need me."

"Where are you going? This is your house."

"Which kind of proves I'm not running away, doesn't it?" He doesn't wait for me to respond before opening the door and walking out.

My heart shatters as I watch him leave. What the hell am I doing? Why am I pushing him away? I really screwed up this time. I rush to the door but he's already driving away.

What did I do? I was so worried about Miles leaving me that I pushed him away.

But instead of ending us, he asked for time to cool down. Miles is not the boy who threw me away years ago. He's a man trying to prove how much he cares for me. And I keep on making him jump higher fences.

No more. It's my turn to make the jump.

Chapter 34

I don't need the Raider brothers to cheer me up. I need Hazel."

MILES

Eli parks his massive SUV at the entrance to the boardwalk and all of us Raider brothers pile out.

"Can we skip whatever this is? I'm not in the mood."

I'm not in the mood for anything. I've barely heard from Hazel since I stormed out of my house three days ago. She hasn't answered any of my calls. And her only response to my numerous messages was, ***I need to think. I'll be in touch soon.***

Needs to think? Without me? Don't I factor into her decisions? The man she loves. But apparently doesn't want to love. Fucking ouch.

I'm giving her what she wants -- some space to think. Too bad she doesn't realize I'd give her anything she wants. But I never promised not to message her. I need to make certain she's okay. It's a living, breathing, pulsing need inside of me.

Jaxon purses his lips. "I'm not in the mood either but no one ever considers my feelings."

Rhett throws an arm over his shoulders. "Because you'd crawl into a cave and never come out if we let you."

"Wrong. My wife wouldn't let me crawl into a cave. I've asked."

Despite how black my mood is, I chuckle at Jaxon. He seriously would prefer to never interact with other people for the rest of his life. Even if the other people are his brothers. Blossom has tried to bring him out of his shell, but there's a limit to how much his wife can do.

"Why do all of my brothers bitch and moan whenever we have a Raider brothers outing?" Eli asks.

Kai's hand shoots into the air. "I don't!"

"Me either." Zane elbows me. "And this one usually doesn't bitch and moan but he's still in the wooing stage."

Wooing stage? I've wooed, and I've wooed. I don't know if I can woo anymore. I'm all wooed out.

Eli rubs his hands together. "Which is why we're having a Raider brothers outing to cheer him up."

"I don't need cheering up."

I need Hazel to answer my calls. I need her to admit she loves me. I need her to give this second chance a real chance. Dive in, Blaze. I promise to catch you.

Jaxon pushes his glasses up his nose as he studies me. "Even I know you're lying."

I give him the finger.

"Everyone, stop acting like a smuggler in love with a mermaid who rejected him," Eli orders. "We're here to have fun."

"And take Miles's mind off how he ruined his second chance with Hazel," Zane adds.

I snarl at him. "I didn't ruin anything."

Did I storm off? Yes. But I made it clear to Hazel that we're not over. I didn't destroy us in a fit of rage. Which is what I feared would happen if I stayed.

"You've been moping around the distillery for the past three days."

"I don't mope."

"Really?" Rhett lifts his eyebrow. "Dakota threatened to transfer all incoming calls to your number and you told her to go ahead."

I shrug. "I was trying to help."

Zane barks out a laugh. "You didn't realize what she said until the first call came in."

Kai shakes his head. "Some poor woman searching for a job and you told her there was no sense working since life was over."

I scowl. "I never said anything of the sort."

"But you are depressed," Jaxon declares.

"I'm not depressed."

He fiddles with his glasses. "You haven't been surfing all week. You yelled at Zane when he asked to borrow your stapler."

"It's a good stapler," I mutter.

"And I found you listening to sad songs when I left last night."

Kai laughs. "Was he listening to Taylor Swift again?"

I glare at him. "Do not make fun of Taylor Swift. She's a goddess who has more talent in her little pinkie than you do in your entire body."

"Whoa!" He throws up his hands and backs away. "He really is depressed."

I stomp toward him. "I'll show you depressed."

Rhett steps in front of me. "No beating up your brother."

"Why not? We're outside. We're not at work. And he deserves it."

"Because violence isn't the answer."

I cross my arms over my chest. "Really? And you didn't throw a bowling shoe at my head because I was, quote, 'being a little shit and you were over it'?"

"You little shit. Do you have my missing bowling shoe?"

I debate lying. I've been hiding his bowling shoe from him since he was in high school. It hasn't been easy since we lived in the same house for years but I can be tricky if the occasion calls for it. And even when the occasion doesn't.

"Maybe."

Rhett dives for me but Eli shackles his wrist to stop him. "No beating up your brother."

Rhett's nostrils flare. "He stole my bowling shoe and kept it hidden for a decade. He deserves it."

I feign buffing my nails on my t-shirt. "Personally, I think I deserve to be crowned the king of the prank wars."

"King of the pain in my ass," Rhett mutters.

Jaxon clears his throat. "Less than ten minutes until we were reduced to name calling. Can I go home now?"

"Nope. We're going surfing."

My mouth gapes open at Eli's announcement. My brothers have never wanted to surf with me. And, trust me, I've tried to get them interested. The closest anyone's come is Jaxon, who rowed every morning while I surfed when we were in high school.

"But none of you know how to surf," I finally manage to say.

Eli grins. "Which is why you're going to teach us."

I frown. "But I don't have my teaching equipment anymore."

"Shit, dude. Were you robbed?" Kai asks.

"Robbed? Why do you think I was robbed?"

"Because there's no other way you'd ever let your surfing equipment go," Zane answers.

"Wrong. I sold it."

Kai's jaw drops to the ground while Zane feigns cleaning out his ear. "What did he say? I think my ears are blocked."

"He said!" Kai shouts at him. "He sold his teaching equipment!"

I might as well get all of this over now. My brothers will act like drama queens and then the teasing will begin. I'm already over it.

"I put the surf shack up for sale."

Kai clutches his head. "I feel dizzy. I think I'm going to faint."

I roll my eyes. "Drama queen."

"This is…" Kai scratches his chin. "I honestly don't know what to say."

"Really?" Jaxon studies him. "You don't know what to say? This is highly unusual."

"Actually." Kai clears his throat. "I do know what to say. Have you lost your mind?"

"I—"

He throws up a hand. "Not done yet. You love that shack. Why the hell would you sell it?"

I shrug. "It was time. It's not as if I'm giving up surfing. But I don't have time to give lessons anymore."

"No time to play with the pretty women who take surfing lessons?" Zane waggles his eyebrows.

I grunt. "You're the player. Not me."

"Not anymore. I'm off the market. I've got a baby and a woman. I'm fulfilled."

I frown. I want to be fulfilled. I want the woman I love living with me. And maybe a baby as well. Not now, but soon.

"I never expected in a million years you'd sell the shack," Eli says.

"What do you mean? I asked if you were okay with me selling the shack." I own the shack but since Eli helped me pay for the renovations after the hurricane destroyed my previous shack, I wanted his permission before selling.

He shrugs. "I thought it was a rhetorical question."

"I asked you for the number of your realtor."

"I think we should say goodbye to the shack before you sell it," Rhett suggests.

"Excellent idea." Kai rubs his hands together. "I'll get the moonshine."

"I'll get the snacks," Zane adds.

They start to rush away but I yell, "Stop! We are not having a party and trashing the shack when it's for sale."

Kai scowls. "Why do you assume we'd trash it?"

"Because I've known you your entire life and you don't know how to stay out of trouble once the moonshine is flowing. Need I remind you of the Great Puking Disaster?"

He shivers. "No need. I'm not the same person. Harper keeps me in line now."

I open up my arms. "Harper's not here."

"Wrong." He points to the beach where Harper is standing with the rest of the partners of the Raider brothers.

"What are they doing here?"

Eli drops an arm around my shoulders. "Aren't you happy to see your sisters-in-law?"

I grunt. I love all of them but being around the women reminds me of what I don't have with me – the woman I love.

He squeezes my shoulder. "Keep watching."

I frown but I do as he says. And I'm glad I do when Hazel steps out from the back of the group and walks to the front.

"Hazel is joining us?"

"This is her show." Eli drops his arm and nudges me forward.

No need to nudge, big brother. I'm going already. I kick off my shoes before stepping onto the beach. I forget all about my shoes as I make my way to Hazel as fast as I can.

"What are you doing here?"

She bites her bottom lip and stares up at me from beneath her lashes. Is she nervous? There's no need for her to be nervous. "I have a surprise for you."

"I love surprises."

"I hope you'll love this one."

I grasp her hand. "If it involves you, I'll love it."

Chapter 35

Brothers are pains in the ass even when they're not your brothers.

Hazel

"This is the best idea," Sadie squeals.

I chew on my bottom lip. "It's not going overboard?"

Scarlett snorts. "You told the man you love you don't trust him to stick around. This is not going overboard."

"I didn't say those words." She lifts an eyebrow and I sigh. "Fine. I pretty much said those words."

Sadie motions to the surf shack. "Thus, the grand gesture."

I frown as I watch the flurry of activity happening around the shack. Balloons are being blown up, strings of festive lights are being strung up, and funny signs are being hung up.

"This is too much. What if he doesn't want the surf shack anymore?"

Sadie scrunches up her nose. "This is weird. What happened to my overconfident sister?"

I point to Scarlett. "She's right there."

Sadie elbows me. "I meant you. Ms. I Will Have My Own Business, I Don't Care What Anyone Says."

I shrug. "I don't own my business anymore. I officially start at *Hideaway Haven Resort* on Monday."

I can't make up my mind how to feel about my new job. Excited? Sure. I won't get the chance to work with NFL players with any other job. Sad? That too. I'm going to miss my cute little practice.

Scarlett wraps an arm around my shoulders. "I'm proud of you. You didn't give up on your dream to be a physical therapist. Trust me. I know how hard it is to hang onto your dreams as a girl in this family."

Sadie nods. "As do I."

Dakota and Blossom hurry to us. "Rhett messaged. They're nearly at the boardwalk now."

"Time to get into place," Blossom adds.

I study the shack, which is hardly a shack anymore. It's more of a mini beach house now. Will Miles like it? My stomach gurgles and I slap a hand over it to calm it down.

Sadie threads her arm through mine. "Let's go."

We follow Dakota, Blossom, Paisley, Harper, and Sloane as they march through the sand to the beach near the boardwalk. By the time we arrive, the Raider brothers are already on the boardwalk. Guessing by the way they keep shoving each other, they're giving each other shit. Nothing new there.

Sloane herds me to the back of the group. "Stay hidden until I give you the signal."

I duck behind my sisters to watch. The group of brothers turns their attention to us and Harper waves to them.

"It's time," Sloane urges.

What's the worst thing that could happen? I'll humiliate myself in front of the entire island. I can handle humiliation. It wouldn't be the first time.

I step out from behind the group and make my way to the front. Miles spots me. He kicks off his shoes before hurrying toward me.

"What are you doing here?"

I bite my bottom lip and gaze up at him from beneath my lashes. "I have a surprise for you."

"I love surprises."

"I hope you'll love this one."

He grasps my hand. "If it involves you, I'll love it."

"Really? You're not still mad at me?"

He snorts. "Guessing by the thousand messages I've sent you in the past three days, I'm not mad anymore."

"I wouldn't say it was a thousand messages."

He grins before clearing his throat and wiping all mirth from his face. "I'm sorry. I overreacted. It's my job to support you. I shouldn't have pushed you to accept the position at the resort. If you want to accept the job at the VA hospital, you have my support."

"Well, crap. I guess I shouldn't have accepted the position at the resort."

His blue eyes sparkle as a smile spreads across his face. "You took the position at the resort?"

"Hudson made me an offer I couldn't refuse."

"You're staying?" I nod. "Whoop! This is the best surprise!"

He grasps my hips and lifts me in the air but I tap his shoulder. "My job situation isn't the surprise."

"It's not?"

"Nope."

"What's the surprise?"

"You'll have to let me down so I can show you."

He drops me to the ground. "Oof!"

"Oops." He steadies me with his hands on my shoulders. "Sorry. I didn't mean to drop you."

He totally did. Miles is a little kid when it comes to surprises. His excitement pulses in the air. This is why I wanted to surprise him. Not because I need to do some grand gesture. But because it makes him happy and I want to make the man I love happy.

I hold out my hand. "Let's go."

He threads his fingers through mine. "Lead me away, Blaze."

I giggle. "Where shall I lead you? To the haunted cave?"

He shivers. "Do not make fun. Smuggler's Grotto is seriously haunted."

"The only people haunting the grotto are your brothers."

"No. I swear I heard Margaret Hale yelling at the pirate Black Jack."

Of course, he did. Because his brothers made a spooky recording and played it in the grotto. But I don't have time to argue about the Lover's Curse now. We're nearly upon the surf shack.

"Close your eyes."

"If anyone kicks me in the balls while my eyes are closed, I'm exacting revenge."

"Don't be a baby. Close your eyes."

I wait until his eyes are closed before continuing toward the shack. I stop a few feet away.

"Okay. You can open your eyes now."

His eyes fly open and he scans the area. His brow wrinkles. "We're at my surf shack."

I motion to the *Miles Beach House* sign. "Not your surf shack anymore."

He steps closer. "This can't be my beach house. I'm selling the shack. In fact, I got an offer yesterday."

"Guess who made the offer?" I tap my chest.

"You made the offer? But why?"

I roll my eyes. "Duh. You love this shack. You were only selling it to prove to me you were serious about staying on the island."

He scratches his beard. "Figured me out, did you?"

"Of course. I know you. I love you."

"You love me?"

I can nod. I already said the words. He knows I love him. There's no reason to be scared. And yet, my body is frozen in place.

He palms my neck and draws me near until his body heat surrounds me. He leans down and whispers in my ear, "There's no reason to be frightened. I've got you, Blaze. I'm not going anywhere. You have my word. I've learned from my mistakes.

I was a fool to not come running back to you the second after I returned from Hawaii. I don't plan to spend another minute without you, let alone several years."

I melt into his arms. "I love you, surfer boy."

"And I love you, Blaze."

His lips mold to mine and I open for him. He thrusts his tongue into my mouth and I moan as his wild ocean taste hits me. It's addictive. And I don't ever plan to kick the habit. This man is mine and I'm not letting him go. If he tries to leave me again, I'm clinging to him like a barnacle on a boat.

The crowd bursts into applause. There's clapping and catcalling until Miles wrenches his lips from mine.

"Let's get rid of them and celebrate our love alone with just the two of us."

As much as his idea appeals, it's not happening. There's no way to get rid of the Raider brothers once they're at a party. And this is a party.

Kai slaps Miles on his back as he passes us, carrying a bottle. "Told you we were drinking moonshine at the shack today."

Zane holds up a bag of chips. "And eating."

Miles groans. "There's food and drink. We're never getting rid of my brothers now."

"There's more than food and drink." I tug his hand. "Let me show you the rest of your surprise."

"There's more?"

I fling the door of the shack open. "Ta-da!"

He scans the room and his eyes widen. "Holy smugglers. This is amazing. It really is a beach house."

"A mini beach house."

The sand has been replaced with hardwood floors. The kitchen has been spruced up to include some shelving. I already added some plates and mugs. And where there once were rows upon rows of surfing equipment is now a little living area with a sofa and some chairs.

"I can't believe you did all this work in three days."

"I had help." I never could have pulled off this surprise without his brothers. It's amazing how well they can keep a secret when they have an incentive. I doubt Miles will be happy with the incentive I offered.

Miles steers me toward the living area. "I'm looking forward to christening the sofa."

I drag my feet. "Not now. Your entire family is here."

"They'll leave if we ignore them."

"Um…"

He sniffs. "Do I smell fire?"

"It's the barbecue."

He lifts his eyebrows. "The barbecue?"

"For the party, I promised your brothers for helping me."

He mutters some swear words under his breath. "They're not leaving, are they?"

I shake my head. "The christening of the sofa will have to wait."

He tugs on one of my curls. "I've waited years for you to admit you still love me. I can wait a few hours until my brothers are gone."

"Are you two done making out?" Zane shouts into the shack. "I need to get the meat out of the refrigerator."

"Yes!" I answer at the same time Miles yells no.

Zane skips inside. "Now you know how it feels to be interrupted."

Miles glares at him. "I've never interrupted you and Sloane."

Zane grabs the tray of hamburgers and hot dogs from the refrigerator. "I didn't say you did."

"You…"

I shackle Miles's wrist before he goes after his brother. "This is a party. No fighting."

"Fine," he pouts. "But you owe me."

I wiggle my eyebrows. "However will I pay?"

He palms my cheeks. "We have the rest of our lives to figure out a payment system."

I grin. "Yes, we do because you are not leaving me again. I won't let you."

"Don't worry, my bloodthirsty Blaze. I don't plan on leaving you until the last breath leaves my body."

"I love you, surfer boy."

"And I love you." His mouth melds to mine and I melt into him. It's only been three days, but I missed my surfer boy. I wrap my arms around him and he presses his hard length into my stomach. My panties dampen in response. Maybe it is time to fool around on the sofa after all.

"Stop making out!" Kai shouts through the window.

Miles tears his mouth from mine. "I love you, but I hate my brothers."

I bury my face in his chest to hide my laughter. This is where I belong. Where I've always belonged. I just needed to get over myself first. Mission accomplished.

Chapter 36

Home is not always where you expect it to be.

A FEW WEEKS LATER

Miles

I use the key Hazel gave me to enter her apartment. "Blaze! You home?"

"In the kitchen."

I freeze at the entrance and lift my hands in the air. "I'm unarmed. Don't hurt me."

She scowls at me. "It's a screwdriver. Not a weapon."

"I don't know. The last time you used a screwdriver, police showed up."

"It wasn't the police. It was the fire department. Which was completely over the top, considering there was barely any smoke coming out of the toaster."

"But the toaster was toast."

"Ha! Ha! Pun intended."

"Why do you have the screwdriver out again?"

She waves it at me. "Don't you mean how did I find the screwdriver?"

Confession. I hid all the tools after the last fiasco. I don't have a problem with women making repairs. I do have a problem with Hazel thinking a hammer is a good implement to separate frozen hamburger patties. It's not.

I shrug. "Was it hard to find?"

"You hid the entire toolbox in a box under the bed labeled tax documents."

I scratch my beard. "I did? Doesn't sound like me."

She snorts. "It totally sounds like you. And I sure as mermaid didn't label a box tax documents."

I cringe. "No. You put your tax documents in a plastic bag and then dump them at your accountant with a smile. I can't believe she hasn't quit yet."

"She loves a challenge."

"No one loves a challenge that much."

"Whatever. We've established you hid the tools from me." She wags the screwdriver at me. "Never again, surfer boy. Never again."

"I can agree to not hide the tools." Throwing them away isn't hiding, right? "If you tell me why you've got the screwdriver out again."

"It's not a big deal. One of the stove knobs is loose. I'm fixing it."

Her stove is gas. My heart lodges in my throat. I rush to the stove. "What have you done? Did you call the fire department already?"

"You are such a drama queen. We don't need the fire department. I'm merely disassembling the knob to tighten it."

I snatch the screwdriver from her. "No, you're not. You could accidentally open the gas valve too far or crack the plastic housing, causing a gas leak."

She rolls her eyes. "I'm not going to cause a gas leak. It's a little knob. No big deal."

"Which is what you said about the cabinet light, the wobbly ceiling fan, the blender. Need I go on?"

"You make it sound as if my place is falling apart."

"Blaze, your place is falling apart." I throw the screwdriver on the counter before grasping her hands. "Why don't you move into my house?"

She drops her chin to her chest but not before I notice the scowl. Does she hate my place? She prefers to stay at her place but I thought she just wanted to have her stuff close by.

I pinch her chin and lift her head until she meets my gaze. "What?"

"What? What?"

"Don't try to bullshit a bullshitter. It'll never work."

She blows a raspberry. "I don't want to hurt your feelings."

"Do you love me?"

"Of course, I do."

I smile. "Then, nothing you can say will hurt my feelings."

"Don't be too sure," she mutters.

I drag her to the living room and sit on the sofa before drawing her onto my lap. She straddles me with a huff.

"Why are you huffing? You enjoy this position." I waggle my eyebrows.

"Because sitting down means this is a serious conversation, and I seriously don't want to hurt your feelings."

I palm her neck and lean my forehead against hers. "I told you, Blaze. You can't hurt my feelings as long as your love for me hasn't died."

"I can still hurt your feelings. You got all butthurt when I told Eli I'd met some famous footballer before you."

"I wasn't butthurt."

"You said – and I'm quoting here – I can't believe you told Eli before me. You wound me."

I squeeze her neck. "Tell me why you don't want to move into my house. If it's too quick, I'll understand."

"Too quick?" She snorts. "We've been in love for over a decade. Quick has jumped aboard a smuggler's ship and high-tailed it into the seven seas."

"Okay." I nod. "It's not too quick. You prefer to stay in your place. I'll ask Eli if he has a recommendation for a contractor. I prefer to live in a house, but I can adjust."

"I don't want to stay here. It's too small. And there's no yard, should we ever decide to have children."

"Children?" I lift my eyebrow. "Is that what this is about? Did you decide you don't want children after all?"

She slaps my shoulder. "No. I still want children. Not six boys for sure. But one or two."

"I'm stumped. You don't want to stay here, but you don't want to live in my house. What's wrong with my house?"

Her nose scrunches up. "This is the part where your feelings might get hurt."

"You hate my house?" I shrug. "It's a house. You don't have to love it. We can buy a new one."

"Whoa. Hold your mermaids. Buying a new house together is a big deal."

"I love you. You love me. Living together is the next step. Unless you want to get married first. Damnit. I screwed up. You want to get married before we officially live together. Not a problem. We can make this happen."

"You were supposed to hold your mermaids. Not jump on top of one and go for a ride."

I rub a hand down my face. "I'm seriously confused, Blaze. You're going to have to explain things for me. Explain it like I'm a kindergartner who didn't show up for the first two weeks of classes."

"Fine." When she pauses, I squeeze her neck. "I don't want to live in your house because there are too many bad memories associated with it."

"Bad memories?"

"I may have accidentally, totally not on purpose, happened to watch you walk into your house with a floozy from Mermaid Karaoke a time or two."

I wince. I shouldn't be surprised. I've staked out Hazel's place a few times over the years as well. No matter how much I tried to avoid her, I was drawn to her. All those years wasted. Because I was an idiot. No more.

"Okay. We won't stay in my house any longer. I'll contact Jade today. We should probably have an idea what we're searching for. How many bedrooms, bathrooms, etc."

Her mouth drops open. “Are you serious?”

“Yes.”

“You’re not mad?”

“Nope, and I’m not butthurt either. I understand. I don’t want any reminders of the years we spent apart, either. I should have realized earlier.”

“But a new house? Can we afford it?”

I smirk. “With the money I won in the Raider Brothers prank war, we have a substantial down payment.”

She rolls her eyes. “You just had to mention you won, didn’t you?”

“It’s important my woman understands I’m a winner.”

She barks out a laugh. “You’re lucky I love you.”

“I am and I’m ready to show you how much I love you.” I punch my hips and my hard cock hits her core.

She moans. “I guess we’ll call the realtor later.”

I stand with her in my arms. “Much later.”

“Much later? Sounds like a challenge.”

“I love you, my little challenge-obsessed screwdriver-wielding woman.”

“Good. Because I love you and I’m never letting you go.”

Her arms tighten around my shoulders. She’s crazy if she thinks I’ll ever let her go. But she can wrap those arms as tight around me as she wants. After all, in her arms is where I belong.

D.E. Haggerty

Love and Laughter in Every Chapter

About the author

D.E. Haggerty is an American who has spent the majority of her adult life abroad. She has lived in Istanbul, various places throughout Germany, and currently finds herself in The Hague. She has been a military policewoman, a lawyer, a B&B owner/operator and now a writer.

Printed in Dunstable, United Kingdom

79133087R00163